"My date has nothing to do with you!"

"It has everything to do with me," Hunter said. "If I'm the one who has to rescue you from something you can't handle."

"*You* rescue me?" He'd been nowhere in sight for most of the day. "I don't need a—a protector," Pernelle snapped.

"Huh!" he grunted. "So next time you're in too deep and call for help, I'm to leave you to get on with it, am I?"

"I won't call out," she retorted and, with more temper than prudence, continued, "I'm twenty-two now. It's time I knew more of the world." Then, at the sudden demonical look that came into Hunter's eyes as he came a few paces nearer, she wished she hadn't added anything....

Jessica Steele first tried her hand at writing romance novels at her husband's encouragement two years after they were married. She fondly remembers the day her first novel was accepted for publication. "Peter mopped me up, and neither of us cooked that night," she recalls. "We went out to dinner." She and her husband live in a hundred-year-old cottage in Worcestershire, and they've traveled to many fascinating places—including China, Japan, Mexico and Denmark—that make wonderful settings for her books.

Books by Jessica Steele

HARLEQUIN ROMANCE
3114—HIDDEN HEART
3126—A FIRST TIME FOR EVERYTHING
3156—FLIGHT OF DISCOVERY
3173—WITHOUT KNOWING WHY
3203—RUNAWAY FROM LOVE
3215—HIS WOMAN

HARLEQUIN PRESENTS
717—RUTHLESS IN ALL
725—GALLANT ANTAGONIST
749—BOND OF VENGEANCE
766—NO HOLDS BARRED
767—FACADE
836—A PROMISE TO DISHONOUR

BAD NEIGHBOURS
Jessica Steele

Harlequin Books

TORONTO • NEW YORK • LONDON
AMSTERDAM • PARIS • SYDNEY • HAMBURG
STOCKHOLM • ATHENS • TOKYO • MILAN
MADRID • WARSAW • BUDAPEST • AUCKLAND

Original hardcover edition published in 1991
by Mills & Boon Limited

ISBN 0-373-03227-7

Harlequin Romance first edition October 1992

BAD NEIGHBOURS

CHAPTER ONE

QUIET, sleepy Chumleigh Edge, with its air of serenity, its wealth of trees—huge oaks and horse-chestnuts—its village green and old stone houses, was, Pernelle thought, one of the most lovely places on earth.

She had thought so last December when she had driven through the centre of the Wiltshire village to half a mile outside, to see Myrtle Cottage with a view to buying it. Hardly daring to hope that the outskirts of the village would retain such loveliness, Pernelle had been utterly enchanted to observe that not only had the area where Myrtle Cottage stood retained the loveliness, but it exceeded it.

Myrtle Cottage, with its adjoining though smaller Primrose Cottage, was built in the most idyllic spot. The two semi-detached cottages stood as one in their own grounds, with no other house in sight. At the front were long lawns which ended with a hedge at the front and, with similar long lawns at the back, a screen of trees some distance beyond at the rear.

The pair of cottages, she had soon learned, had in years gone by been one dwelling until it had been inherited by two brothers by the name of Goodwin. They could have sold the property and divided the proceeds, but, with the property being in such an exquisite spot, Pernelle could fully see why the brothers had decided to partition it and turn it into two dwellings. That both properties were without a garage was neither here nor there, since there was standing space on the gravel drive for several cars.

With the one property sectioned off by a dividing wall, Myrtle Cottage and Primrose Cottage evolved, with both properties having thick, stout outer walls. One brother must have inherited a two-thirds share and the other brother the remaining third, Pernelle realised, for Myrtle Cottage was twice the size of Primrose Cottage.

The brothers were dead now and the properties had passed on to their wives. The senior Mrs Goodwin had recently moved into a nursing home, and it was her home, Myrtle Cottage, which was up for sale.

Pernelle looked over the cottage and instantly fell in love with it, winced at the price, but still wanted it. That was last December. Today, the first Saturday in June, was moving in day. Pernelle had waved goodbye to her mother and stepfather who had helped her move in, then took a turn about her sitting-room. She then went to look out of the window on to her overgrown lawn. There was a yard-wide strip of gravel that ran across the immediate front and rear of the two properties and which had clearly been used as a short cut to each other's houses by the relatives, but, beyond that yard-wide strip, a two-foot-high box hedge running from the top to the bottom of the lawn separated one garden from the other.

The next-door garden, she saw at once, was immaculate, and her ire started to rise. She stamped down on it hard—her neighbour was plainly 'not in residence' this weekend. Pernelle mastered any tart thought that would have followed. Hadn't she decided when she had bought this place that she was not going to allow any sourness to spoil her pleasure?

She had known the moment she had finished viewing Myrtle Cottage that she wanted it. And so, after deep thought and discussions with her mother and a building society over a mortgage, and, after a 'neck or nothing' gulp at what she was taking on, she had decided she must have it. She would buy Myrtle Cottage. Enchanting Myrtle Cottage with its one very large bedroom and one average-sized bedroom, and bathroom upstairs. Delightful Myrtle Cottage with its kitchen, dining-room and very large sitting-room downstairs.

The only trouble was, though, that the window she now stared through on this moving-in day was the *average*-sized sitting-room window of the one average-sized bedroom *only*, dining-room*less* cottage, which was smaller by a half.

She, who had gulped when she'd decided to buy it, and who had today moved in, had moved not into Myrtle Cottage but Primrose Cottage—the cottage next door. She had, in fact, been gazumped!

For the first time uncaring of the view of the beautiful rolling hills in the distance, Pernelle recalled the Saturday morning when, with her head a-buzz with plans for moving into Myrtle Cottage, she had called in to the estate agents' on some small matter.

'I've been trying to contact you!' Rufus Sayer, a partner in the firm, exclaimed, and proceeded first to put a damper on her plans, and then to absolutely flatten them, by telling her that someone had, that morning, put in a higher bid for Myrtle Cottage.

'But Mr Goodwin's already accepted my offer on his mother's behalf!' she protested. 'He can't...' She broke off when the look on Rufus Sayer's face said otherwise.

'I'm afraid he can,' he informed her regretfully. 'Up until the moment both you and his mother have signed the contract, he, acting for her, is perfectly at liberty to sell to the highest bidder.'

'But...' Pernelle protested vigorously, but all to no avail.

There was not a thing that could be done, Rufus Sayer told her. Mrs Goodwin was elderly and had reached a stage where she could no longer cope on her own. She was now comfortably installed in an expensive nursing home, but her son, in the hope that she would live for a good many years yet, took the view that the more he could make on the sale of Myrtle Cottage, the more comfortable her remaining years would continue to be.

At the realisation, Pernelle's initial anger dipped. But, as she saw her dreams of owning the enchanting cottage turning to ashes, she tried desperately to hang on to it.

'How much more did this other buyer offer—can you tell me?' she asked. She had no idea if it was ethical or not for him to do so, but, having pushed herself to the financial limit to make her initial offer, she felt stubbornly disinclined to give up without a fight—even if common sense did decree that she just couldn't afford to go any higher. 'Perhaps I can up my offer a little more,' she went on, but Rufus Sayer, a presentable man of about thirty, was shaking his head before she had finished speaking.

'It wouldn't do any good, Miss Richards,' he told her, again looking regretful. 'Mr Tremaine has seen Myrtle Cottage and has instructed his solicitors to go ahead with the purchase.'

Just like that! Pernelle's lovely dark brown eyes widened in surprise. 'You're saying that, having seen it, this man—Mr Tremaine—is determined to have it, price no object?' she demanded.

'I'm afraid so,' he replied, and added. 'Maybe I'm doing Mr Goodwin a disservice, but I happen to know that any higher offer made will be topped by Mr Tremaine through his solicitor.'

That, Pernelle thought glumly, is *determined*! 'I'm glad he's got so much money,' she said waspishly. Then, realising that Rufus Sayer was piggy-in-the-middle in all of this and that it wasn't his fault if somebody else had seen Myrtle Cottage and, as she had, fallen in love with it and all the beauty that surrounded it, she relented to comment, albeit disappointedly, 'I don't suppose I can blame Mrs Tremaine for thinking Myrtle Cottage and its setting little short of Shangri-La.'

'Er—from what I've gathered from his solicitors, Mr Tremaine isn't married,' Mr Sayer told her.

'He's a bachelor?'

'It would seem so.'

Pernelle was silent for a moment or two as she cogitated on this Mr Tremaine who was a bachelor and who was, by the sound of it, so busy that he employed others—in this case solicitors—to do all his chasing about for him. 'Does he come from around here?' she asked, knowing quite well that what she should do was accept defeat and go on her way.

'He lives in London, actually,' Rufus Sayer obliged.

'Chumleigh Edge must really have got to him, for him to want to move out of London,' she remarked, still having trouble in accepting that she had lost Myrtle Cottage, and upset enough to want to vent her disappointed feelings on someone—the unknown Mr Tremaine fitting the bill nicely.

She was therefore little short of staggered when Rufus Sayer revealed, 'Oh, he's not moving from his London home.' And, almost admiringly, 'He's much too busy to be able to spend more than just the occasional weekend in our quiet backwater.'

'He's not . . . !' Pernelle gasped, but, recovering fast as what he had just said fully sank in, 'Then it's a pity this Mr Tremaine couldn't find a cottage in some other "backwater" than Chumleigh Edge!' she commented crossly, and started to become so incensed that she left the estate agents' barely able to nod in acknowledgement of Rufus Sayer's eye-to-business comment that if another similar cottage should come on their books . . .

She was still furious as, later, she let herself into the house she had grown up in. She didn't want another cottage—she wanted Myrtle Cottage, and some big shot from London had outbid her!

Too angry to sit down, she paced the sitting-room, knowing she should ring her mother and stepfather and tell them of this latest and unexpected and unpalatable development, but feeling she should try to cool down first before she did so.

Her mother had been widowed eighteen years ago, when Pernelle had been four, and although her mother, recently married to Bruce Lewis, was supremely happy with him, Pernelle didn't want her worrying on her daughter's behalf.

Half an hour went by and Pernelle was still fuming. She might, she thought, have been able to accept more graciously what Rufus Sayer had told her had this Tremaine man wanted to make Myrtle Cottage his full-time home. But weekend cottage! *Occasional weekend cottage* at that—it was enough to boil the blood of even the most saintly!

Why couldn't he buy a cottage somewhere else? Why pick on her cottage? Why, for that matter, since it seemed that he needed an occasional weekend away from London, couldn't the wretched man put up at a hotel? The country was positively littered with them.

Not at Chumleigh Edge, beautiful Chumleigh Edge, though, she thought, her initial outrage at last starting to fade. Chumleigh Edge didn't boast a hotel, just one shop, one church, and one pub.

It was another half-hour before Pernelle went over and picked up the phone to make her call to her mother. By then she had been all over everything again—including how the idea of becoming a property-owner had originally been born.

She and her mother lived in a pleasant house in the pleasant and sizeable town of East Durnley. Pernelle had gone to work for Mike Yolland Plastics straight from secretarial college, while her mother worked as a day receptionist at one of the local hotels.

It was through her work that Stella Richards had met Bruce Lewis who, on business in East Durnley occasionally—but more frequently of late—stayed at the hotel. He came from Yeovil in Somerset, and was without family apart from a twin sister who lived in Cornwall.

Pernelle knew that, although her parent was very particular, she sometimes accepted an invitation out. But there had never been anything very serious until that one evening when her mother asked, 'Are you doing anything this Friday?'

'I've told Julian I'd...' Pernelle broke off. There was something in her mother's expression, a new something, a hint perhaps of some suppressed excitement was the nearest she could come to it, and yet, at the same time, her parent looked serious. 'What's...' wrong, she had been going to say, but, looking at her mother, she somehow knew that not a thing was wrong. Indeed, if her instincts weren't playing her false, everything was very much all right! 'Julian won't mind if I tell him I can't make it,' she at once changed tack, that hint of excitement in her mother rubbing off on her. Julian Collins was more friend than boyfriend and might as easily discuss with her which other girl he should take to the jazz concert if she couldn't go.

'If you're sure,' her mother smiled, then seemed to take a big breath. 'There's somebody I should like you to meet,' she admitted.

Instantly a smile beamed from Pernelle. 'Not this Bruce I've heard so much about?' she guessed.

'Have I mentioned him before?'

'*Moth-er!*' Pernelle teased, and so Bruce Lewis came to dinner, and if there was a hint of excitement about Stella Richards, then that same look was about him as well. His eyes followed her mother wherever in the room she went, Pernelle observed, and while seeming comfortable with her, he also appeared delighted each time he heard her voice.

There were daily phone calls in the week after Bruce returned to Yeovil. And then came the Monday evening, after Bruce had forsaken the hotel in favour of staying with them in their home for the weekend, that her mother told her that Bruce had asked her to marry him.

Pernelle only just saved herself from hurling herself at her mother in a loving hug—something uncertain in her mother's expression causing her to halt. 'What did you tell him?' she asked instead.

'You don't—mind?' Stella Richards asked a shade hesitatingly, and at that, as it quickly hit Pernelle that her mother must be holding back on her behalf, she did launch herself at her and give her a big hug.

'Dope!' she scolded. 'Why would I mind?'

'Your—father.'

Pernelle could barely remember her father, who had been killed in a car accident. 'I'm sure he'd want you to be as happy as I want you to be,' she told her mother sincerely.

'It will mean changes—my marrying Bruce,' Stella Richards warned.

'Great!' laughed Pernelle, wanting her mother to be happy and not worried—now of all times.

'You'll come to Yeovil to live with Bruce and me, then?'

'Ah!' murmured Pernelle, and set to with her mother to work out the first snag—and every one that cropped up thereafter.

For a start, she quite liked where she now lived. She very much liked her employer and his family and got on well with them. She enjoyed her job in East Durnley very much too, and although she might have considered giving up her job and her friends to move away, she instinctively felt that her mother and new husband deserved to start their marriage on their own.

'Would you mind very much if I stayed in East Durnley?' she asked.

'Oh, love,' Stella Richards said worriedly. 'I know you'll think it quaint and everything, but—but—well, I'd rather thought of selling the house.'

'I should think so too!' Pernelle replied stoutly, never having thought about it, but having grown aware over the years that her mother had a thing about financial security. Clearly, the dear love wanted the security of some capital behind her when she took the step into a second marriage. 'I'll have no trouble whatever in finding a flat to rent, I'm...'

'You'll do no such thing!' her mother surprised her by declaring. And it was at her instigation, with Bruce fully supporting her action, that she insisted that Pernelle should buy a small property of her own, and decreed that the deposit would come from the sale of the house.

Pernelle dialled her mother's Yeovil number and, as she began to seethe again about that man Tremaine, she again tried for calm at what she had to tell her parent about the small property she had thought was hers.

'What? I don't believe it!' was her mother's initial reaction, and after several minutes of protesting, 'Oh, darling. I'm so sorry. You really fell in love with Myrtle Cottage, didn't you?'

'It can't be helped.' Pernelle hoped she sounded philosophical and not downright furious, as she felt each time she thought of it. 'Naturally I'm disappointed. As you know, Chumleigh Edge particularly appealed to me, but...'

'It more than appealed to you. Oh, what rotten luck!' her mother commiserated.

'Not to worry,' Pernelle said brightly. 'Rufus Sayer has said he'll let me know if anything similar comes in.'

'Huh!' her mother sniffed, then offered, 'Well, I'm glad I didn't put our house on his books. It's as well it hasn't sold yet, though—at least you haven't got to move out in a hurry.'

January gave way to February, but it was early March before a buyer for the house Pernelle had grown up in was found. Fortunately the new people did not want to move in for some months yet—which gave her more breathing space.

She had looked at several smaller properties but had seen nothing that came anywhere near to what she was looking for. She realised that she had lovely Myrtle Cottage, and exquisite Chumleigh Edge, to thank for that.

Her mother returned to East Durnley and stayed over-night whenever Bruce had business in that area, and Pernelle was always pleased to see them. Towards the end of April she paid a visit to them in Yeovil and had a pleasant weekend with them. Not that they did a lot, the weekend consisting mainly of talking, talking and eating, more talking, and Pernelle, because of a next-door neighbour's hip problem, taking Arthur, the rough-haired Jack Russell terrier, for a long walk.

She drove back from Yeovil having satisfied herself that things were as they should be in that her mother had never looked happier, and, as she neared East Durnley, and her mother and Bruce faded from her mind, she started to think of other matters.

She had still not found anywhere to live yet, but as a stray thought of work tomorrow crept into her mind, worrying about where she would live when the new people moved in did not for once occupy prime space in her head.

Business was not going well at Mike Yolland Plastics. Poor Mike was worried to death about his cash flow problems. Robbing Peter to pay Paul had nothing on it as he juggled to keep his head above water. The fact, though, that if matters went on like this for very much longer she would have neither home nor job seemed in-consequential in the light of his worries.

Her secretarial job with Mike had been her one and only job, and with the firm being a new one she had seen it grow. She knew Mike's wife, Zena, and had baby-sat with their two children Tom and Rebecca on the rare occasions that they went out. She liked the family and had over the last few years come to be treated like one of them. So it was only natural, she supposed, that Mike's worries during that week should become hers too.

'What you need is an extra backer,' she declared when on Wednesday, still wading in financial treacle, he informed her that the bank had already been on the phone before she'd got there.

'I wish!' he replied.

By Friday, however, some people who owed *him* money, quite a lot of it, paid up, and that particular crisis was weathered. But it had been a fraught week—so much so that when Saturday morning arrived Pernelle felt more in need of a blow of fresh air than tackling any of her usual Saturday morning chores.

She took a quick look around her already neat-as-a-new-pin home, and wasted no more time. Soon she was out in her car and was leaving the town of East Durnley behind her. She did not drive very far, however, no more than five or six miles, when, as if the charming village pulled her, she found that she was motoring slowly through Chumleigh Edge.

I could have lived here, but for that man Tremaine, she thought solemnly, having never forgotten his name, nor the unfairness that he was living where she wanted to live, but only at weekends. Correction—only on the occasional weekend!

She motored on, out of the village itself, until, when a right fork would have taken her away from Myrtle Cottage, her car seemed to have a will of its own and turned left.

She was still driving slowly, but slowed down even more as she neared the pair of semi-detached cottages. The setting was still beautiful, but the garden of Primrose Cottage seemed strangely neglected somehow—but Primrose Cottage did not concern her just then. What were they doing to beautiful Myrtle Cottage?

Alarm chased through her as she pulled up at the bottom on the double gates of the property and opened the car window for a better look. There was a heap of builders' material on the driveway, which, as her heart sank, meant only one thing to Pernelle. Myrtle Cottage was about to be extensively altered and, in her opinion, absolutely ruined!

'Oh, no!' she gasped aloud, though she had no idea that any sound had escaped her until, while her eyes were glued to the cottage, she suddenly discovered that she had company. A man, a tall man, somewhere in his mid-thirties, had, by the look of it, returned from a walk. He had appeared from the rear of her car and was about to open the gates and go through when he halted to turn and look aloofly down at her.

'Yes?' he enquired crisply, clearly a man who expected straight answers.

As he stared at her, though, so Pernelle stared back at him. His eyes were dark blue, she noted, so dark as to be almost black, and they had already done a speedy if thorough scrutiny of her long thick black hair, dainty features and flawless complexion. His own hair was thick and dark, and he had the merest sprinkling of attractive silver at his temples.

But his look had become sharp, and it seemed to Pernelle as if he was for all the world daring her to object to what he, and his builder, were intending to do to beautiful Myrtle Cottage. And that was when Pernelle's past disappointment and present horror at what she envisaged merged and boiled over into anger.

Who did he think he was, the—the usurper! She was totally unused to being so arrogantly regarded, and she tilted her chin an arrogant fraction too, before she let go with a heartfelt, 'Going to ruin it, I see, Tremaine!'

That she appeared to know his name had no effect on him whatsoever, though it was plain that nobody ever gave *him* the uppity treatment! Plain, too, that he did not care for it. Though when it came to put-down one-liners he was king, she very soon discovered.

'We must have met on one of my very rare off-nights,' he drawled coolly.

'We have *never* met!' Pernelle erupted.

'Then who might you be?' he rapped back before she could draw breath.

'I'm Pernelle Richards!' she snapped furiously, but saw at once that her name meant nothing to him. 'The person you cheated out of Myrtle Cottage!' she was angry enough to hurl at him.

'Cheated?' he echoed, but by then Pernelle had decided it was utterly beneath her to stay and argue with him.

With her head still as much in the air as possible as she searched for first gear, she started up her car and drove away, wishing she had never driven in the direction of Myrtle Cottage, and had never pulled up. Perhaps it was hiding her head in the sand, but she wouldn't be feeling half so churned up inside as she was now if she hadn't seen for herself the evidence that the new owner was going to spoil it beyond recognition.

While her anger remained, Pernelle felt quite justified in calling him a cheat. Only later, when she had cooled down, did she start to think that in calling him a cheat to his face the way she had done she might perhaps have been going a little too far. Even so, it was better to call him a cheat to his face than behind his back, she decided, though was not too sorry that she was never going to see him again.

In that surmise, though, she was to have doubts before the following week was out. Oddly, having met the man Tremaine, having seen him, she was finding it extremely difficult to get what she reluctantly acknowledged was his attractive face out of her mind. Of course it wasn't every day that she got so furious at what someone was doing to a lovely old stone building—not to mention the memory of past events—that she really went to town and called that someone a cheat, but she was glad to get to work on Monday and have something else to concentrate her thoughts on.

She had been at work a couple of hours, though, when Rufus Sayer, the estate agent she had dealt with over Myrtle Cottage, telephoned her. 'I told you I'd let you know if another cottage like Myrtle Cottage came on to my books,' he began. 'I've just been out to measure up something that will suit you down to the ground.'

'Oh, yes?' Pernelle enquired carefully, still in her heart of hearts wanting Myrtle Cottage and no other.

'You'll be thrilled and delighted when you know where it is!' he almost chortled in his selling pitch.

'Where is it?' she obliged, and at his answer, at once felt her pulses start to stir.

'Chumleigh Edge.'

'Chumleigh Edge?' she exclaimed. 'Where in Chumleigh Edge?'

'Do you remember Primrose Cottage? It's right next...'

'Primrose Cottage? Not the one next door to Myrtle Cottage?'

'Yes! Now isn't that lucky?' he said, and went on to tell her how at nine sharp that morning Mr Goodwin, the same Mr Goodwin who had acted for his mother when she had decided to sell Myrtle Cottage, had rung him to say that he was now acting on behalf of his aunt, the owner of Primrose Cottage. She had apparently been finding life exceedingly lonely without her sister-in-law living next door. Things had come to a head, apparently, when she had had a fall and had been unable to get up. But for the laundry man calling that day, she had realised, she would have been in a great deal of trouble. A vacancy now existed in the same nursing home that the Myrtle Cottage Mrs Goodwin was in, and she, missing her sister-in-law too, had finally prevailed on her to join her. 'I'll take you round to view it in your lunch hour if you'd like me to,' he ended.

But Pernelle wasn't so sure, and hesitated. 'I've got a busy lunch hour today,' she replied, having planned to work through part of it, though knowing she could have altered her plan if she really wanted to. 'I'll be in touch,' she told him, and put the phone down—to be plagued from then until she left the office that evening by asking herself what on earth she was playing at. Cottages in Chumleigh Edge didn't come up that often, for goodness' sake!

By the time Pernelle reached her home she had faced the fact that what was really bothering her was having Tremaine for a neighbour. For a few more hours the charms of Chumleigh Edge tugged at her. But, as her mother's offer of the deposit for any suitable property had never been withdrawn, Pernelle knew she was weakening when at about eight o'clock that evening she picked up the phone and rang her mother.

Primrose Cottage, when Pernelle viewed it the next day, was not, as she'd known, as big as Myrtle Cottage. Nor was it in such a good state of repair as Myrtle

Cottage, and it in no way came up to Myrtle Cottage, but it had potential. But because it was not as large as its neighbour, and because of its need of complete re-decoration, the asking price was considerably cheaper.

Pernelle walked around the downstairs sitting-room and kitchen again. Upstairs was a bedroom and a bathroom. She looked out through the rear window at the screen of trees, and at once started to get happy vibes. Gradually the feel of the place started to take over. That night she rang her mother again.

'Did you go to see it?' was Stella Lewis's first excited question.

'I did.'

'And...'

'It wants a lot doing to it. Every room wants decorating and...'

'Did you like it?' was what her mother wanted to know. 'It's in a fantastic spot.'

'It's in a gorgeous spot,' Pernelle could do no other than agree. 'And I could—love it there,' she added honestly. 'But...'

But?' her mother queried.

Pernelle had told her about her brush with Tremaine, though not that she had called him a cheat. 'What about *him*?' she asked.

'Him?'

'My neighbour.'

'From what you've said, he'll only be there at weekends—and only occasionally at that,' Stella Lewis pointed out.

'That's true,' Pernelle agreed slowly.

'And I can't see, if he's so busy that he can only make his retreat on the occasional weekend, that he'll hang on to Myrtle Cottage for much longer,' Stella added, to cheer Pernelle up some more.

'That's a point,' Pernelle replied, and rang off to ponder—should she then, rather than purchase Primrose Cottage, wait for Myrtle Cottage to come on to the market again?

She decided against that when she recalled how it appeared, on a more detailed inspection over the hedge today, that Tremaine was having a large garage built at the side of his property. That, plus any other modernisation he was having done, was bound to take any future asking price way beyond her means. She'd pushed herself to her financial limits to offer for it before, she recalled.

The next day she went into the estate agents' and put in a firm bid for Primrose Cottage, but she did not make the mistake again of thinking Primrose Cottage was hers until the day both she and Mrs Goodwin had signed the contract.

She saw Tremaine only once again, and that was two weeks after she had called him a cheat. Her mother and Bruce were up for the weekend, itemising what furniture was to go to Yeovil and what would ultimately find a home in Primrose Cottage. It was Saturday afternoon when all three of them took a drive over, and Tremaine was on his way out.

Had things been different, Pernelle might have introduced herself as his new neighbour and introduced her mother and stepfather, but she didn't, in any case, get the chance, for Tremaine didn't so much as glance her way.

With her chin in the air she went up the path to the front door of Primrose Cottage and went in. She had not set eyes on him since. Everything went smoothly after that. She moved out of her old home that Saturday—the new people were moving in on Monday.

With a start, she came to, saw the beautiful rolling hills in the distance and wondered how, for what must have been a good half an hour, she had been staring out at her lovely view without actually seeing it while she allowed her thoughts to play back.

She came away from the window without pausing to wonder when the charm that Primrose Cottage too held had started to weave the same spell over her that the next-door cottage had. All she knew was that as soon as that contract had been signed, ensuring that no one would then be able to stop the sale with a higher bid, she had relaxed and allowed herself to grow fond of the place—though, she at last owned, she had had a warm feeling for the cottage from the beginning.

As with everything, though, she mused as she went through to the kitchen at the rear to make herself a warm drink, there had to be one fly in the ointment.

This particular fly was her arrogant next-door neighbour. Still, looking on the bright side, she had the place to herself from Mondays to Fridays, and he wasn't there this weekend either. With luck maybe he wouldn't come Wiltshire way next weekend either.

In fact, if she was really, really outstandingly lucky, she might never have to see his lordly, arrogant person ever again!

CHAPTER TWO

THE first thing Pernelle did when she awoke on Sunday was to get out of bed and go to her bedroom window, open it, and fling it wide. A sigh of pure rapture left her. Heaven was Primrose Cottage!

Ignoring for the moment the fact that every room in her new home was going to have to be redecorated before it would be truly liveable in, she stared contentedly out at her view.

A few minutes later she pulled her gaze away from the distant hills and began to notice the scenery nearer to home. For a start, her garden was going to need some attention soon. It was really quite amazing that in such a short space of time as the few months since Mrs Goodwin had left, the garden should have returned— well, almost—to the wild.

Though taming the garden was not one of her first priorities, Pernelle reflected, her gaze drawn, if unwillingly, over the neatly trimmed top of the dividing two-foot-high hedge into her neighbour's garden.

For a man who was never there, Mr Tremaine kept his garden very spruce, she saw. But she had no liking for the man and was quite happily certain that not one blade of grass would dare to defy him and grow where it should not.

By the look of it Tremaine hadn't arrived during the night, she observed, for no smart, last-word-in-elegance Jaguar stood on the driveway, as it had the last time she had clapped eyes on him. Not that he'd any need now

24

to leave his car on the drive, she realised, recalling that among whatever other alterations, he had also had a large double garage built.

She couldn't see the garage from where she was, of course—well, not unless she hung out of her bedroom window, and she had no intention of doing that—just in case, unheard, he had driven down during the night. All builders' rubble and impedimenta had been cleared away now, but Pernelle could clearly recall that, along the building line of the cottages, Tremaine had built his garage. Not by so much as half an inch did it jut out, but, built in the same pale grey stone, it blended in beautifully with the cottages and looked so much part and parcel of the scene that if you didn't know differently you'd have thought the garage had always been there.

Pernelle came away from the window musing that Tremaine must have something of an aesthetic eye, and that she had been more than a little unfair to accuse him of being about to ruin it.

She went downstairs to make herself a cup of tea and felt quite chastened for several minutes. But all that changed when she remembered that, but for him, she would be the owner-occupier of Myrtle Cottage.

Any sour thoughts that might have accompanied that memory were negated, though, when she thought of how Primrose Cottage was hers, and how she was going to make it beautiful.

Half an hour later her telephone rang. It was her mother. 'I knew you'd be up!' she exclaimed.

'What's the matter—couldn't you sleep?' teased Pernelle—it wasn't seven o'clock yet.

'So what are you going to do today?'

'Before or after I put everything away?'

'It will take you a couple of weeks or more to do that,' was her mother's opinion. They chatted idly for ten minutes or so, then her mother rang off. Pernelle got showered and dressed and made a start on unpacking the vast amount of china and paraphernalia which her mother, since there was little that her home with Bruce lacked, had insisted she would need.

Pernelle had a busy Sunday. She spent a busy day at her office on Monday, Tuesday and Wednesday and came home each evening to unpack and find homes for yet more china. She arrived home on Thursday and saw that a gardener had arrived next door and was mowing her neighbour's lawn. So that was how it was done—you hired somebody!

Had she that sort of money, Pernelle might have gone and had a word, but, as she had decided to do her own decorating and so afford a rather expensive carpet she wanted for her sitting-room, a gardener would have to wait until one of her Premium Bonds came up. Meantime, she'd get round to her garden the first chance she had.

'My mother was right,' she told Mike when he took a break from his business worries on Friday afternoon and asked how she was getting on. 'She said it would take forever to get everything unpacked.'

'You're still at it?'

'I'm tackling the last tea-chest tonight,' she replied, and, more because he had been so worried lately, his cash-flow problems again peaking, she attempted to keep his mind anxiety-free for another minute as she told him how tomorrow she intended to start scraping the old wallpaper off the sitting-room walls prior to redecorating.

'I'd have thought you'd have done all that before you moved in,' Mike remarked.

'In an ideal world, I would have. But with the new people wanting to move into our other house last Monday, and the Goodwins' solicitors not allowing me to have the keys before completion day, I didn't get the chance,' she explained, and, their brief respite over, they got down to work again.

Pernelle went home that night to finish the last of her unpacking, while her employer, she knew, went home to worry about how he was going to keep his head above the yet deeper financial water he was in this time.

Saturday dawned a beautiful sunny day. Pernelle threw wide all the windows in her home and, never more contented in the beauty and tranquillity of her surroundings, within the next hour she was hard at work with a wallpaper scraper.

An hour later, having discovered that the previous occupants had gone in for papering *on top* of the old paper, she realised that any idea she had had of having all the paper stripped off the wall by lunchtime was a vast underestimation.

At about eleven o'clock that morning she put down her paper-scraper and put through an urgent call to her mother. 'Are there any shortcuts to paper-stripping?' she asked hopefully.

'Having trouble?'

'There must be five layers of paper on the walls at least—each and every one of them stuck down with superglue,' Pernelle replied.

Her mother sympathised for a while, then went away to ask Bruce's advice. 'You could try sponging it down with a strong solution of detergent,' her parent returned to tell her.

First I need a drink, Pernelle thought, and having perspired freely, she went into her kitchen and poured herself a glass of lemonade. Picking up a kitchen chair, she took it outside and decided to have a ten-minute break in her back garden.

Only a minute later, however, while she was contemplating the weeds and thigh-high grass, she heard sounds which, if her intelligence wasn't playing her false, denoted that her next-door neighbour had decided to pay Myrtle Cottage one of his occasional visits.

Instinctively she made to get up and go indoors. Then, abruptly, she halted. What was she running away for, for goodness' sake—she *lived* here!

She heard the sound of her neighbour's garage doors being opened, heard his car being driven in and then the garage doors being closed. Almost as if to make her claim on her property, she sat there stubbornly, but she was about to relax at the thought that her neighbour would now go in by the front door when, to her discomfiture, he suddenly appeared round the back.

As before, she instinctively wanted to be indoors, and was in fact on her feet before the stubbornness returned. 'Good morning,' she greeted the tall dark-haired man stiffly. She saw his aloof glance go over her, from her pulled-back hair down her long length of leg and sandal-clad toes, and she was overwhelmingly aware of what a sketch she must look—all legs and arms in her shorts that had seen better days and her T-shirt.

Who dressed up to paper-strip walls on a boiling hot day, anyhow? she was thinking, having belatedly realised that she was grimy into the bargain. Stripping off wallpaper was not the cleanest job in the world, she had discovered.

At last, however, the man, who was looking at her as though he couldn't believe it, drew his gaze away from her sweaty, leggy form, though not to return her greeting, but to state tersely, 'I trust you'll be a quiet neighbour.'

That was all she needed. 'You've no children, then?' she queried in her best superior voice, well aware that he was a bachelor.

He was sharp, though, she gave him full credit for that. For instead of asking what the devil she was talking about, as well he might have, he was instantly on the attack, to demand, 'Have you?'

'I'm not married!' she hurled back.

'That,' he snarled, 'means nothing,' and, clearly having better things to do than spend the rest of the day bandying words with her, he turned round, unlocked the rear door to his property and went in.

Pernelle glared at his newly painted back door and, although she was ready to go in herself by then, she obstinately stayed exactly where she was for another five minutes.

When she did go in, however, she soon realised why it was that he had thought to voice his trust that she would be a quiet neighbour. For—something she had not even thought about, as there had not been anyone inside the next-door property on her previous visits— she could hear more or less every sound he made when he was in the next-door room. From her kitchen, at any rate, she could hear him moving around in his kitchen. So OK, she'd got her kitchen window open—as he had his open—but she would swear she had actually heard his fridge door being slammed shut just then.

Oh, lovely, she thought, without much joy, and re-called from the time she had viewed Myrtle Cottage that as his sitting-room shared the same wall as her sitting-room, then that same wall separated his main bedroom from hers. Terrific, she thought, but as she got over her shock and hoped that he used his other bedroom, the one on the outside wall end, she recalled that his bathroom was on that wall too, so at least she'd be spared knowing each time he took a bath.

The Goodwin brothers could never have heard of soundproofing when they had partitioned the property, Pernelle reflected as she paper-stripped her way through the rest of that Saturday. Whimsically she wondered if on wet days they shouted out any messages to each other rather than take the short cut where the lawn-dividing hedge ended and the yard-wide strip of gravel was.

At any event, if Tremaine had come down to Myrtle Cottage for a bit of peace and quiet this weekend, she hoped he wasn't taking his ease in his sitting-room. Because, as she had heard some of his movements when he was in the next room, he must therefore be able to hear her. Pernelle smiled happily as she worked.

It was around nine o'clock that evening when she removed the final tiny bit of wallpaper from the walls. Aching in every limb, she went and had a hot bath, washed her hair, and shortly afterwards fell into bed.

Out of consideration for the neighbour she did not begin sizing her sitting-room walls until eight o'clock on Sunday morning. Whether or not her neighbour was in the habit of leaving his weekend cottage at around eleven on a Sunday morning, though, she had no idea. But at eleven she saw his car going down the drive. It did not totally surprise her that she did not see him again that weekend.

She was leaving for work on Monday when she saw a wiry-looking woman of about fifty-five get off her bike and push her cycle through the double gates of Myrtle Cottage.

'Good morning!' Pernelle greeted her when the woman came further up the gravelled drive and looked across. 'I'm afraid Mr Tremaine isn't in,' she volunteered.

'Oh, I know,' the woman replied cheerfully. 'I'm Mrs Moore from the village. I always come on a Monday and do for Mr Tremaine when he's been down of a weekend.' What method she had of knowing when he'd been down, Pernelle didn't get to hear, as the open-faced Mrs Moore paused, then commented, 'I'd heard that a young lady had moved into Gladys Goodwin's old place. I hope you'll like it here.'

'Thank you,' Pernelle smiled, and told her, 'My name's Pernelle Richards, and I love it here—it's beautiful.'

'It's certainly that all right,' Mrs Moore beamed, and seemed disposed for a long chat, but Pernelle had a job she wanted to be at for nine o'clock, so she wished the woman a smiling goodbye and got into her car.

The week turned out to be a very busy week for Pernelle. Mike Yolland was still dreadfully worried about money and was very much afraid he stood to lose his company if he couldn't soon do something about it, and he had plainly been doing some very in-depth thinking over the weekend.

'Fourth light of my life, thank you,' he greeted her when she went in and, for about the third time since they had known each other, he dropped a light kiss on her cheek.

Pernelle was quite happy that his wife and two children preceded her in the 'light of his life' pecking order, but she was nevertheless puzzled. 'What did I do?' she asked.

'I've been going mad wondering how to keep the firm afloat,' he began. 'Then on Saturday something you said ages ago came back to me and, instead of dismissing it out of hand as unaffordable, I suddenly began to wonder—was it? I've spent most of my time since then checking and re-checking figures, and I reckon I can just do it.'

'Do it?' she questioned, and, still in a fog, although she was usually much quicker on the uptake than this, 'What was it I said?'

'You said,' he smiled, 'that what I needed was an extra backer. And, Pernelle, you're right. Though since nobody around here is likely to back us, it seems to me that my best plan is to get in touch with some of the large London-based finance houses. Get your notepad out, there's a love.'

Pernelle felt it was a big responsibility to have the initial idea laid at her door. But she *had* said something of the sort, she remembered vaguely, and as that week moved on she began to feel quite excited. Some companies they phoned first, and were told to write in with details of the project they had in mind.

While working hard at the office, Pernelle was working equally hard at home. Chris Farmer, a friend of a friend, had rung up for a date on Tuesday, but she had much too much on to consider going out in the evenings.

By Friday she had almost completed the painting and wallpapering of her sitting-room. By Friday, too, Mike Yolland was eagerly scanning the post for a reply. All he'd so far got was a few acknowledgements of his communication, and one from a firm advising that they would put his application in front of their committee at the next meeting.

'It looks as though it's going to take months before I'm going to get a decision from anywhere!' he complained in his anxiety.

'Well, we are asking for a lot of money,' Pernelle attempted to soothe him.

'It's a lot to us, but peanuts to them,' he replied, and considering that she was seldom if ever late, she had the present stress he was under to thank for his anxious, 'Can you be sure to be here by nine on Monday? I've a meeting with the accountants first thing, and that London company, Edgars, said they'd let us know as early as they could on Monday—they might ring and...'

'I'll be here at eight forty-five, I promise,' she butted in with a smile.

When at mid-afternoon the phone on her desk rang, she had started to grow as uptight as her employer. When the call proved to be Chris Farmer again asking her out the following evening, she realised that she could do with a night out.

'I'd like that,' she replied, and could not resist a glow of pride as she added, 'I live at Chumleigh Edge now,' and gave him the rest of her address.

She went home that night having worked hard at her job all week, having put in double time in soothing wherever she could and generally doing her bit to help her boss keep his sanity. But, like magic, all the stresses and strain of that day started to fall away from her when she reached the outskirts of Chumleigh Edge. She motored through the village and, as always, thought it beautiful.

She drove up to her cottage, got out of her car and opened the double gates at the bottom of the drive. By the time she had driven through, parked her car and gone down the drive to close the gates again, she felt whole once more. She had started to adore her lovely Primrose Cottage.

At eleven-thirty that night she surveyed her newly decorated, only just completed sitting-room. She had helped her mother redecorate in the past, but this was the first time she'd tackled anything on her own, and she was rather pleased with her efforts. The wallpaper she had chosen was of the palest green with the palest pink Regency stripe going through. Her carpet, when it was laid on Monday, would be pale green, and her pink curtains, when she put them up, would be tied back with pink and green striped silk cord. Until she could afford some new furniture, she was happy to use her mother's large and wide beige and pink settee, which was still in good condition.

Pernelle went to bed tired, but was up early, refreshed and eager to get started on stripping the wallpaper in her kitchen. It was another warm day, but the sky was overcast, promising rain.

It did not rain, however, but more cloud appeared on her horizon when, no mistaking that her neighbour had arrived for the weekend, she heard him moving about next door. That made it two weekends on the trot! Perhaps, dared she hope, it meant he would not be around next weekend, or the weekend after that? Her good humour surfaced, and she smiled at the thought that she certainly couldn't be doing with him coming to his occasional weekend cottage *every* weekend—as if she'd got any say in the matter!

At twenty past six she came away from her absorption with the paper-stripping job in hand, to suddenly remember that she had a date with Chris Farmer at seven o'clock. Galvanised into action of another sort, she quickly got down from the foldaway steps she had been standing on, and raced to take a bath, wash her hair and file yet another broken nail down.

At one minute to seven she was dressed in the nearest thing to hand, which happened to be a quite classy-looking silk dress of a warm red colour. A quick glance out of her bedroom window showed that her date had just drawn up in his car.

Pernelle picked up her bag and ran lightly down the stairs. She went out of the front door, saw Chris at the bottom of the gate just about to come through, then forgot him entirely as she noticed that her neighbour was standing on his gravelled drive, watching her.

Last Saturday he had seen her when she must have been looking her very worst. She had no idea why it should bother her, but she felt pleased that this Saturday he should see her when she was looking as smart as paint.

'Good evening,' she felt pleased enough to pass a cool time of day—and was ignored for her trouble.

Rats, she thought, and did a little ignoring of her own as she turned her attention to the man who was her escort for the evening. 'You're looking good enough to eat!' Chris greeted her. She smiled, and got into his car.

She kept her eyes staring resolutely straight ahead as the car went by Myrtle Cottage. But, most oddly, all the way to East Durnley, while she chatted idly to Chris, her thoughts were back in Chumleigh Edge.

Oh, how she wished she hadn't spoken to the wretched man! To ignore her the way he had! Who the devil did he think he was anyway? Well, she'd make sure it would be a long time before she spoke to him again.

'I thought we'd have a drink at the Globe first, then have dinner somewhere,' said Chris.

'That sounds fine.' Pernelle smiled, and went back to thinking about her tall and decidedly unneighbourly neighbour.

Well, one thing was for sure, he'd be able to have his dinner in peace this evening without the sound of her paper-scraper on the kitchen wall. Then she remembered that he, unlike her, had a dining-room and, in a lull in the conversation with Chris, she fell to wondering if Tremaine ate his solitary dinner in his kitchen or whether he stepped across the hall with his meal into his dining-room.

All at once, though, Pernelle was quite jolted by the thought that, since he'd been standing near his garage, had he been on his way out for the evening too? Was he eating neither in his kitchen nor his dining-room, but taking some lovely female out somewhere? Somehow Pernelle just knew that any girl he took out would just have to be 'lovely'. And when she found she was frowning at the thought, she was immediately ridiculing herself that it bothered her what his companion looked like. As if she cared! For goodness' sake, as if she was jolted in the slightest that he most likely had a date that evening too! 'I haven't been to the Globe in an age,' she informed her companion.

As evenings out went, her evening out with Chris Farmer was about average. She quite liked him, and he was easy enough to talk to, but by ten o'clock she wouldn't have minded at all had he suggested taking her back to Primrose Cottage. It was not very complimentary to him, she had to admit, but while he was going into some intricate details of his job, her thoughts were more on the walls she was going to finish scraping tomorrow and, if she had time, give a coating of size.

At just after eleven he pulled his car up outside Primrose Cottage and, as Pernelle turned to thank him for a pleasant evening, she discovered that he had amorous tendencies. Reading the signs that he was about to kiss her, she averted her head, and his kiss landed on her cheek.

'Super dinner!' she trotted out lightly and, reaching for the door handle, 'Goodnight,' she bade him, and got out of the car.

To her surprise he got out of the car too. 'Don't I get to come in for coffee?' he persisted.

Pernelle quickly, though without apparent haste, put herself on the other side of her double gates. 'I've only just moved in and I haven't got the place straight yet,' she replied, still keeping her tone light. 'Another time, perhaps,' she attempted to soothe any hurt feelings.

'I'll keep you to that,' he answered, and earned a good mark for not proving tiresome as he got back into his car and drove off.

Pernelle went up the drive to her cottage, noting that, apart from the street lamp at her back, both Primrose Cottage and Myrtle Cottage were in complete darkness. Was Tremaine in bed and asleep, or was he out? Where, she didn't care to speculate. Or—something she had only just thought of—had she driven him out with her scraping? Had he in fact got so fed up that he had gone back to London for some peace and quiet?

She had ample evidence that Chumleigh Edge still had the pleasure of his company when at eight-thirty the next morning her phone rang—and it was him!

'Confound it, woman!' assaulted her ears before she could get in so much as a 'Hello'. 'Can't you, like normal people, have a lie-in on Sunday?'

'You've fetched me down a ladder just to ask me that?' Pernelle exploded, exaggerating the size of her foldaway steps in her annoyance at his way of speaking to her.

'Haven't you finished *yet*?' was his next complaint.

'I've got another two rooms to go at when I've finished this one!' she stormed, and slammed the phone down, and ten minutes later had thought of several much better replies.

It's always the way, she fumed, but, temper-assisted, she made great strides in her work and by four o'clock that afternoon had completed her paper-stripping and, with a short break for a sandwich, had put a coat of size on the kitchen walls.

Feeling suddenly exhausted, she went upstairs, and was soon afterwards in the bath having a glorious soak when she came to to realise that she had nearly nodded off. Ten minutes later she was bathed, dressed in a fresh T-shirt with a smart pair of floral dungarees on top and a pair of sandals. What she needed, she decided, was some fresh air. She'd been so busy since she'd moved in that there had been no time to go and take a look around 'her' village.

The sky was overcast but the weather was still close when, with her door key in her dungarees pocket, Pernelle effortlessly pulled the front door of Primrose Cottage shut behind her. For a moment she halted and pondered about the door catch and the easiness of closing the door. Was the catch too free? She wondered about the security the door lock afforded, but when she stretched out a hand and tested the door, it was quite secure and no amount of pushing at it disturbed its firmness.

She turned from her experimentations, then saw that Tremaine's car was standing on his drive. Good, perhaps that meant he was on the point of leaving. So, feeling cheerful—him and his 'Haven't you finished *yet*?'—she swung happily down her drive and went exploring.

Joy filled her as she turned down a lane and walked in the direction of the village proper. Was she lucky or was she lucky? 'Good afternoon,' she replied to a friendly greeting as she went. Reaching the post office-cum-shop, she paused to read some of the postcard advertisements in the window. Someone was offering a home ironing service at a reasonable rate, she read, there had been a whist drive in the village hall last night, and yoga was taught there every Tuesday. Happy to be part of the small community, even if she did live on the outskirts, she walked on for a while.

She took a right turn after that, then a left, and found she was in open country again. She came to a field where sheep were grazing, and wasn't sure about the country rules of trespass, though she thought if she left no gates open and made sure not to frighten the animals, the farmer might not object to her crossing his land on this, her first experimental day.

It was a large field, the field the sheep were in, but Pernelle was so concerned with watching the sheep to ensure that she was not frightening them that she was unprepared when the rain that had been threatening for a couple of days finally arrived. She had made it across the field and was standing in the next one securing the gate when suddenly the heavens opened.

Somewhat shaken to be caught in such a sudden downpour—her attention had been more on the animals than the weather—Pernelle got herself swiftly together. But her hair was already plastered wetly to her head when all at once she spotted, and took off for, a nearby barn.

She was proud of her sprint, even if it had left her out of breath, for as she rounded the side of the barn and found the wide open doorway, she had made it in record time. No sooner had she leapt inside, though, than her self-congratulatory smile disappeared. For, as she was midway to pulling back her wet hair from her face, she discovered she was not the only one sheltering from the sudden squall.

'You!' she cried accusingly at the very last person she had expected to see there.

Casually his glance flicked over her bedraggled appearance, rested for a brief moment on her heaving bosom, then back up to her rain-washed face. 'It's my fault that it's raining?' he mockingly answered her accusation—and hate suddenly flooded her.

The fact that last night Tremaine had glimpsed her looking almost elegant, was suddenly wiped clean away. All she could remember as she started to hate him was that she had thought he had seen her looking her very worst when he'd come home to Myrtle Cottage and seen her labour, sweaty and grubby, in her old shorts and T-shirt. But now look at her—no make-up, hair plastered to her head, wet through and scared to move because she just *knew* her sandals were going to squelch if she did.

She ignored him totally—not that that seemed to break his heart—and stared out at the still bucketing rain. She hadn't looked at him again, nor would she, but her memory was good, and she had no trouble whatever in recalling that it hadn't looked as though so much as one tiny droplet of rain had fallen on him. Naturally, she fumed sourly, he had seen the rain coming and had reached the barn before the first spot had fallen.

The sky was still emptying when, as an odd sort of tension mounted in her, it suddenly dawned on Pernelle that she was so rain-sodden now as made no difference and that she couldn't get any wetter—well, not much—if she went out and headed for Primrose Cottage this minute. Who the devil cared about squelchy sandals anyhow!

In the next moment Pernelle had taken two steps outside the barn, then, her eyes widening in horror, she froze. Disbelieving, only by some superhuman effort was she able to control the scream of panic that rose to her lips. Though some sound must have escaped, she realised, because Tremaine had moved. Suddenly he was out in the pouring rain too.

Then, his voice a blend of arrogance and mockery, 'Cows!' he scoffed. Pernelle was still standing horrified and belatedly realising she hadn't given cows a thought when she'd been thinking in terms of not frightening the animals—yet here were those very large beasts, absolutely petrifying her. 'Don't tell me the lady's moved into the country, yet she's afraid of cows!' Tremaine drawled, truly enjoying himself, she knew.

His mockery, however, his hateful, vile, arrogant mockery, proved to be just what she needed. He *knew* she was terrified, he just knew! But when she had two choices—stay where she was or go back inside—Pernelle started to get angry. Was there to be no end to the humiliation she had to suffer at his hands? she fumed. And it was then that she discovered that she would not be humiliated—she just would not! She would not, tail between her legs, go back inside that barn!

With more courage than she ever knew she possessed, and on a gulped breath, and without a backward or a sideways glance, Pernelle started walking. She no longer felt the rain as, with her palms perspiring, and a feeling of sickness in her stomach, she neared the herd. They stood unmoving, staring, and she suddenly found herself eyeball to eyeball with one of them—and very nearly faltered in her stride. But, swallowing hard again, she looked away, and forced herself on, on and past them—and, at long last, she made it to the gate that she had come through earlier.

Swiftly she put herself to the other side of the gate and fastened it. Only then, from her safe position, did she glance back at the barn. And she was never more glad then that she had managed to keep her nerve and not sprint those last few yards—it had been a near thing—because Tremaine had been watching her. He had moved further from the barn and, heedless of the rain, was standing there watching her! The swine!

Hate him? She positively loathed him! She turned round and headed for home. Oddly, though, long before she reached Primrose Cottage she suddenly found she was feeling strangely elated! Now why was that? It couldn't have anything to do with *him*—could it?

CHAPTER THREE

HER elation of the previous afternoon had nothing at all to do with Tremaine, Pernelle knew the moment she awakened on Monday morning. She had, in fact, reasoned before going to bed last night that the sole cause for her feeling of elation had come from the unbelievable achievement of facing up to her fear of cows. That fear, she knew, was tied up with, and stemmed from, her mother's fear when, out blackberrying with her one afternoon when Pernelle was a small tot, she had toddled off on her own to do some exploring. Her mother had panicked on discovering she was missing, and her subsequent frantic calling of her name while moving at speed searching for her had in turn alarmed some nearby cows. They had taken off and were heading straight for Pernelle, who was toddling towards the sound of her parent's panic-stricken voice. That panic, coupled with the sight of what seemed mammoth-sized animals running at her, had resulted in trauma.

However, Pernelle, remembering her promise to Mike that she would be at the office at eight forty-five that morning, got out of bed and went downstairs to make a pot of tea.

' She could hear the occasional sound of her neighbour moving around in his kitchen next door, and wasn't sure how she felt about this new development—this fact that he was extending his weekend right up until Monday morning.

A moment later she could only wonder at herself and her thinking. What had got into her, that she should have turned positively cranky where Tremaine was concerned? For heaven's sake, it was his property, he had every right to reside there—all through the week too, if he so desired! For all she knew, he might well be planning to do just that.

Pernelle went and sat at her kitchen table, sipping her tea and pondering on the fact that she had never liked him even before she'd met him. But—she struggled for fairness—given that he had done her out of Myrtle Cottage by outbidding her on the price, would she not have done the same had she the funds?

By the time she had finished her tea Pernelle had started to think that maybe it wasn't so much Tremaine who was the cheat but Mrs Goodwin's son in that, having accepted her offer, he had gone back on it. She then thought of how he wanted as much money as he could get in order to ensure that his mother enjoyed her remaining years to the full—no expense spared. In that context, Pernelle realised that the ethics of it all suddenly no longer seemed to apply.

What did it matter anyhow? she thought as she went back up the stairs to take a shower. She had Primrose Cottage, hadn't she, and had grown to love Primrose Cottage every bit as much as she had fallen in love with Myrtle Cottage?

By the time she had completed her ablutions, her good humour was restored and she was again feeling very pleased with herself to think that yesterday she had confronted her bogey of certain farm animals. That wasn't to say that she would at some future date voluntarily be placing her person in the same field with another herd of cows, but, thanks to Tremaine... Abruptly such thoughts ceased. Why thanks to him? And, come to think of it, why, for goodness' sake, had he been the first person to enter her thoughts when she had woken up that morning?

Pernelle thought she had the answer when she pulled her front door shut behind her and went over to her Metro. No one in her life before had ever aroused the intense emotions he had. She had never hated anyone before, and although she was feeling that emotion less passionately this morning, wasn't it only natural that, having been stirred to such strong emotion, she should be thinking from time to time of the man who had incited such vehemence?

She inserted her ignition key, observed idly that it seemed to have rained heavily during the night, but, with the air fresher for the rain, it looked like being a lovely day.

The lovely day, however, began to fall apart at the seams when, to her dismay, she discovered that her car wouldn't start! 'Oh, no!' she groaned. Nothing had ever gone wrong with it before and, not being at all mechanically minded, she had no idea what she could do to make it go.

She was still turning the ignition on and off and pressing her foot down on the accelerator, when, tall, immaculately business-suited and with briefcase in hand, her neighbour came out of Myrtle Cottage, locked up, and then, seeing her, hearing her frantic attempts to start her vehicle, ignored her and turned his attention to opening up his garage.

In the small time it took for him to drive his elegant Jaguar out of his garage Pernelle had accepted that her wretched car was just *not* going to start. But memory of the stress Mike Yolland was under, his anxiety lest that important call from Edgars was missed, made her feel doubly agitated about getting to work on time.

She had hated Tremaine yesterday afternoon. She doubly hated him that Monday morning. For although he could hear, if not see, that she was in trouble, he had closed his garage doors and was already steering his car down to the double gates at the bottom of his drive.

Swine! she fumed, hating him even more to realise that, when he would have to go through East Durnley and pass right by her place of work to get to the motorway, he was not going to offer her a lift.

He had the double gates open and was back in his car when her loyalty to her boss suddenly overcame her obstinacy to see Tremaine in hell before she'd ask him for a lift. In the next second, having recently became quite good at sprinting, she was sprinting out from her car through the pathway along the front of the two cottages, and down his drive after him.

More hate stirred in her when, having presented herself at the driver's window, she thought he was going to continue to totally ignore her. But, just as her temper went on an upward spiral and she felt angry enough to thump on the glass, he turned arrogantly and looked down his nose at her. How he was capable of doing that when he was in a sitting position, and she standing, was beyond her, but he managed it.

Aware that she couldn't afford to be angry, she controlled her crossness to simmering point when he deliberately forced her to wait before pressing a switch that electronically operated the window and the window slid gracefully down.

Without having the least idea why it should matter, Pernelle was momentarily sidetracked from her panic to be at work on time when his glance went over her, and she was suddenly glad she had chosen to wear a smart suit of lemon linen, the jacket sleeves giving that suit a touch of elegance in that they were just elbow-length. Tremaine's lofty glance didn't linger, but she didn't doubt for a moment that he was recalling the sodden sight he had seen yesterday when she had dashed into that barn.

But, pig that he was, he was leaving it to her to explain what she thought she was doing by delaying him. Pernelle took a controlling breath, then discovered that even if she was quite desperate for a lift, her pride would not allow her to go down on her knees and beg him to take her into East Durnley. For, although she tried hard for a pleasant note, her voice came out sounding quite sharp when she asked, 'Is there any point in appealing to your better nature?'

Dark blue eyes stared arrogantly into hers and he sent her fury into orbit again as, knowing full well what she was asking, she was sure, he aloofly enquired, 'In what respect?'

With the utmost difficulty, Pernelle managed to swallow down her ire. 'I need to be at my office before nine,' she started to spell it out for him, adding what she knew he was completely aware of. 'My car won't start.'

For long pride-crucifying moments she thought he was going to refuse, because he did nothing for an age but just sit there studying her solemn, unsmiling expression. Then, somewhat to her amazement, he demanded, 'Still think I'm a cheat?'

Her mouth fell open in her surprise that, after all these months, he should have remembered that she had introduced herself, 'I'm Pernelle Richards! The person you cheated out of Myrtle Cottage!' It was especially surprising when she considered that it was only that morning that her feelings on that particular matter had calmed sufficiently for her to give fairness a chance and to accept that, with Mr Goodwin after every penny, if Tremaine had not gazumped her then someone else surely would.

But Tremaine seemed to be making something of a study of her parted lips, and Pernelle quickly pulled herself together. She supposed, with more fairness, that an apology was due, but, knowing she would feel totally mortified if Tremaine thought she was only apologising in order to scrounge a lift, she looked him squarely in the eye and answered, a shade stiffly, 'No, I don't.'

For perhaps two seconds more he looked arrogantly back at her, then he clipped, 'Get in!'

Tremaine, she soon found out, was not the most chatty person to ride to work with. Though he did condescend to ask in which direction she wanted to go.

'East Durnley,' she told him. 'You'll pass my office if you're taking the motorway to London.' She thereafter lapsed into silence herself to realise, with a fairness that insisted on raising its irritating head again, that she'd been wrong to fume in advance about Tremaine not offering her a lift when he was passing her place of work.

He hadn't known *then* in which direction her workplace lay. With more of that irritating fairness she discovered that she was *actually* thinking in terms of him being very kind! Well, she didn't know what else she could call it, she reflected, because—not before he'd stirred her to anger, admittedly—he had seemed prepared to give her a lift, wherever it was in Wiltshire that she worked.

Any mellowing of feeling about him on that account, however, very soon evaporated when Mike Yolland Plastics came into view and she pointed to the building and asked her neighbour to pull over.

'You work for Mike Yolland?' he enquired casually.

'I'm his secretary,' she replied, but when he halted the car, and she stepped out, the 'Thanks for the lift' which she'd had ready got buried as her curiosity stirred. 'Do you know him?' she asked.

His answer was to close the door on her. She was still standing there staring, when in the next moment the Jaguar purred off to merge with the rest of the traffic.

Swine! she fumed, and, feeling utterly idiotic and wishing she'd *never*, *ever* asked 'Do you know him?', she went inside the building. Of course he knew Mike, or at least had heard of him!

Pernelle was still smarting at having been made to feel so small when at ten-thirty a grey-faced Mike came in. She did not need any guesses to know that any picture the accountant had painted had been edged in mourning black. 'Did Edgars phone?' was Mike's first question.

'Sorry,' she had to tell him, and what with one thing and another, not to mention her smarting feelings on the subject, she never got round to asking Mike if he knew or had heard of her neighbour Tremaine.

The week that had started off so badly did not improve to any great extent. Pernelle had phoned her usual garage about her car and Nick, one of their mechanics, called at her office for her car keys. He subsequently phoned to say he'd got her car going and that he'd popped the car keys through her letterbox.

'It sounded a bit complicated,' she related to Mike when he asked what the trouble was. 'But, from the sound of it, the distributor got damp with all the rain we had yesterday and in the night.'

'You'll have to get yourself a garage,' was Mike's opinion, and, as Pernelle was thinking that the expense of a garage was something she wasn't ready for yet, the call he had been expecting from Edgars came in.

She saw at once from his defeated expression that his hope of borrowing some money from them had been turned down. She felt heartily sorry for him, but admired him for managing not to crumple, as he courteously thanked the person on the other end for their consideration.

'I'm truly sorry, Mike,' she offered gently when he put the phone down.

'Give me ten minutes,' he said brokenly.

Pernelle went swiftly back to her own office. Grown men didn't cry, but she reckoned Mike was near it. Five minutes later she heard him on the phone to his wife. Five minutes after that he came into Pernelle's office.

'That's some wife I've got,' he announced in less shaky tones. 'According to Zena, we've still got another few irons in the fire. If Nathan Finance turn us down, then there's still Braddon Consolidated and . . .' He broke off, picking the phone up on her desk when it rang. 'It's for you,' he said, and passing the phone over to her, returned to his own office.

The call was from her friend Julian Collins ringing to ask her new home phone number. Fleetingly she thought of how, since she wasn't in the book yet, Tremaine must have been through to directory enquiries to have phoned her that time, then she gave her attention to Julian.

'It's about time we went out for a meal,' he declared.

It seemed, apart from one person in particular, that it was her day to say sorry. 'I'm sorry, Julian, I'm up to my ears in house decorating. I'm a bit busy right now.'

'So when am I going to see this cottage?' he enquired, completely unoffended.

'I'll have a cottage-warming when I've...' she began, then remembered that she had no way of getting home that night. 'Actually, you could see it this evening, and at the same time ferry me home,' she changed tack to tell him, going on to relate how her car had let her down that morning.

'I owe you one,' he replied in his happy-go-lucky way, and went on to remind her of a time, which she'd forgotten about, when she had helped him out with transport.

Good as his word, he picked her up from her office that evening and drove her home to Chumleigh Edge. The carpet fitters had been, leaving the spare house key she had provided on the kitchen table, so Pernelle was pleased that she was able to show Julian her one respectable room in the cottage.

They shared a tray of tea in her sitting-room, but, aware that she wanted to get on, Julian did not stay long. Oddly, she started to feel very low-spirited shortly afterwards. Though, apart from knowing that the way she was feeling had nothing at all to do with Julian, she could find no answer for why she should feel that life was a little—dull.

It was a feeling that persisted throughout that week, and was not helped by Mike Yolland's being in a depressed state too. Chris Farmer rang for a date on Wednesday, but Pernelle could find neither time nor inclination to go out with him, so she put him off. On Thursday she finished redecorating her kitchen, and on Friday, her spirits still no higher than they had been, she started work on her bedroom.

At around nine that evening, however, she heard the click of a gate through her open bedroom window and went to the window to investigate. It was not her gate

that was being opened, though, she discovered, but that
of her neighbour. She saw his Jaguar, saw Tremaine get
in behind the wheel and steer his car up his drive. She
went back to work and—odder than ever—she suddenly
found she was feeling far more cheerful than she had all
week!

Because her bedroom was in such a mess Pernelle spent
the night on her settee, but that feeling of cheerfulness
was still with her when she awoke the next morning. She
sang lightly to herself as she made some tea, then went
upstairs to shower and get on with the job in hand.

Suspecting that Tremaine was using the large bedroom,
the one that shared a wall with hers, she worked as
quietly as she could for the first hour until she heard
him up and about. For the next couple of hours she
worked on solidly, but it was just before eleven, having
returned upstairs after carrying a large plastic bag of
waste out to the dustbin, that she happened to glance
out of the window, just as a smart car pulled up outside
Myrtle Cottage. Her curiosity was stirred when a woman
of about thirty, equally smart-looking, got out of her
car and walked up her neighbour's drive.

Pernelle returned to her labours, but, to confuse her
somewhat, she discovered that she couldn't settle, and
each time she paused to take a breather, she would go
and take a look outside. That car was still there!

At half past one she went and made herself a sandwich
and a drink. She returned at five to two—the car was
still there. Pernelle was painting her bedroom door when
at six o'clock she heard her neighbour's gate click.
Swiftly, though careful to stay out of sight, she looked
through her bedroom window. The woman had decided
to leave, apparently, and, by the weary look of her, would
not be coming back.

Pernelle went and returned to her painting and absolutely refused to think what it was that Tremaine had been up to for *seven* hours, to make his lady friend look so exhausted.

She did not have much more painting to do, but when the door was finished, she suddenly felt restless. Feeling unable to settle all at once, she decided she had done enough for that day and, it being a fine evening, she decided she needed some air.

Pausing only for a quick wash, in next to no time she was securing the back door of her cottage and was walking past her car to the front of her property. She had only taken a couple of steps on to her front drive, though, when she heard a sound that caused her to look over to her left.

Her neighbour was just coming from his garage, she saw. Remembering that the last time she had been in his company he had driven off rather than deign to answer one of her questions, she favoured him with a cold look, observed that he didn't appear impressed by it, and would have gone on—had he not, arrogantly, delayed her.

'You're going for a walk!' It sounded more like an accusation to her ears than an enquiry.

'What of it?' she retorted.

She had her answer in no time when, casting a glance at her thigh-high, weed-choked lawn, he lobbed back at her curtly, 'You'd be better employed in getting busy on your garden!'

The nerve! The utter nerve! 'If you've any *energy* to spare, you can tackle it for me!' she hurled at him, and refusing to wait to see what he made of that, she stuck her nose in the air and sailed on her way.

The cheek of it! she fumed, as she marched in the general direction of the village. OK, so her garden was a mess, an eyesore, but she had so much else she had to concentrate on first. And besides, the odious toad, he didn't do *his* garden himself but paid somebody to do it for him!

Making sure she didn't go into any fields, Pernelle was so incensed she was halfway to the next village before she began to cool down. She turned round and started to return more slowly.

The light was not as good as it had been when she reached Chumleigh Edge, though it was perfectly light enough for her to pause and read the postcard adverts in the post office window.

A gardener was offering his services, she read, before she walked on. But she had a perfectly good lawn-mower—courtesy of her old home—in her shed at the top of her garden, and she'd be hanged if she'd pay out for gardening money she needed for other things. That a scythe would be a more appropriate tool than a lawn-mower to tackle the job was something she wouldn't waste her time thinking about.

What she did have to spend her time thinking about, she discovered the moment she reached her cottage, was what she was going to do about electricity. For on entering her kitchen in the dusk of the evening, she switched on the light switch—and, for no reason she could fathom, blew the lights.

Her first instinct was to get on the phone to her mother, but she was a grown woman now, and her mother had a new life. Apart from which, Pernelle remembered belatedly, her mother and Bruce were spending this weekend visiting Bruce's sister in Cornwall.

Her second instinct was to pop round to her neighbour for assistance. She abruptly cancelled that idea—she'd die sooner. Tremaine just wasn't that sort of a neighbour!

Pernelle thought for a moment or two more, then, recollecting that she'd seen an electrician advertising 'no job too big, no job too small' in the post office window, she found a torch and went out in her car as far as the post office.

When she returned to Primrose Cottage armed with the name Eddie Johns and his phone number, she decided it was a little late to ring him that night.

Bearing in mind, though, that some people appeared to like a lie-in on Sunday mornings—she thumbed her nose through the wall at her neighbour Tremaine—Pernelle held back on Sunday from ringing Mr Johns until nine o'clock.

'Good morning,' she began. 'You won't know me, but I've recently moved into Primrose Cottage, and...'

'Old Mrs Goodwin's place?'

'That's right, yes. And...'

Half an hour later a thin and lively man in his late forties pulled up in a van outside. Fifteen minutes after that he had been all over her cottage making a general inspection.

'Sooo...!' he whistled through his teeth, and revealed, 'This place has never been rewired since the electricity was put in!'

'That's—er—bad?' Pernelle enquired, fearing the worst.

'It's not good,' he confirmed, and went on to tell her that, although he could fix her up with some power, she should most definitely consider having the cottage completely rewired.

'Er—how much is that likely to cost?' she asked tentatively. She couldn't avoid the question, after all.

'Oh, not too much,' he beamed, and got deep into negotiation, during which Pernelle learned that he was so busy that he couldn't possibly start a rewiring job before a week next Monday.

By lunchtime, however, she had the safe temporary electricity supply she needed, but, having accepted Mr Johns' rewiring estimate, she had realised that she was wasting her time in doing any more redecorating until Mr Johns had finished. By the sound of it, the floorboards were going to have to be taken up. Realising that she might as well move back into her bedroom for a week, she realised also that there was more to this buying of old property than she had bargained for.

With the rest of the day free, she looked out of the window at her neglected garden. She knew, without Tremaine's curt observations, that she should be out there doing something—but some inverse kind of pride seemed to make it impossible for her to go and tend to her garden while he was in residence. She wasn't having him thinking she was jumping to do his bidding!

He left on Monday, and Pernelle came home each evening to attempt to do something about her disgraceful garden. One way and another, though, with Mike Yolland having been turned down by Nathan Finance and more worried than ever, she suffered another low-spirited week. When Chris Farmer rang on Friday afternoon and suggested dinner that evening she was again ready for an evening out.

She was getting ready to go out with Chris that night when her phone rang. 'Eddie Johns here,' her caller announced. Her heart sank, as she was sure he was ringing to say he wouldn't be able to start on Monday as promised. 'I've finished the other job I was on sooner than I thought,' he told her jauntily. 'Is it convenient if I start your job first thing in the morning?'

Her heart lifted. The sooner the better, in her opinion. 'That will be fine,' she answered warmly, and from her window she saw a sleek Jaguar pull up. Suddenly she started to feel brighter than she had all week. It was all down to Mr Johns' phone call, she decided.

Her date with Chris Farmer went off well, but when after dinner he began to talk in terms of going on to a nightclub Pernelle had other ideas. East Durnley had two nightclubs—and from what she'd heard, neither had too good a reputation.

'Would you very much mind if I went home now?' she asked, and went on to relate how Mr Johns, the electrician, was coming to start work first thing in the morning.

Her liking for Chris Farmer increased when he at once agreed to take her home. Since, though, she was fairly certain that with the next day being Saturday she wouldn't see Mr Johns much before ten, she was feeling just a tinge guilty at that 'first thing in the morning' when Chris halted his car outside her house.

'I've had a lovely evening,' she told him more warmly than she otherwise might.

'Don't I get to come in?' he queried, turning in his seat, his left arm coming along the back.

'Mr Johns,' she laughed, and was about to reach for the door handle when the headlights of a car pulling up from the opposite direction startled her. Chris chose that moment to place his mouth over hers—and Pernelle was still feeling startled when he moved his body over hers. He had effectively stopped the stationary car's lights from blinding her, but as she twisted her head to one side, she wasn't sure which she preferred. 'Goodnight,' she bade him abruptly, and with more speed than he was prepared for she was out of the car and putting her gates between herself and her escort.

Chris Farmer and his amorous intent went completely out of her mind as she recognised the car that had just pulled up. She turned her back on it and went up her drive. It must be half past eleven if not later, she calculated as she found her key and let herself into Primrose Cottage. Quite obviously Tremaine had been out on the tiles—probably with some woman, she concluded, and went to bed feeling a little out of sorts.

Pernelle was up early the next morning—and was glad of that fact too when, at three minutes past seven, Eddie Johns arrived to start work! She went to the door to let him in, musing that it was no wonder he'd finished his other job ahead of schedule if he started work so early in the morning.

At twelve minutes past seven, while Pernelle strove to hide her anguish, he started ripping her home apart. At fifteen minutes past seven, while Mr Johns was upstairs, he either hit something with a sledgehammer or dropped his metal toolbox from a great height, because suddenly there was a tremendous crash that seemed to rattle the whole cottage.

'Oh, lord!' muttered Pernelle, downstairs in her sitting-room, and was wishing she was going out somewhere if it was going to be like this for the rest of the day—gardening was out while Tremaine was around—when all at once her phone rang. A smile of pure impishness tugged at the corners of her lovely mouth. Think of the devil, she mused, and went to answer it, fairly certain who her caller might be before she'd even picked up the phone.

She was proved right. For, before she could so much as say 'Hello', a voice she would know anywhere blasted her eardrums. 'What the *hell* is going on?' her next-door neighbour thundered.

'It's not my fault if you've got a hangover!' she purred sweetly, and quietly put down the phone. Suddenly she felt good.

That good feeling diminished somewhat when, at just before eleven, she saw Tremaine's date of last Saturday drive up.

Throughout that day Mr Johns was in and out, and sometimes driving off to get something that took half an hour. In between times Pernelle was kept busy plying him with tea and coffee—of which he drank gallons. He was still busily at work, though, when at five-thirty she saw the next-door visitor go down the path to her car.

Pernelle was still watching as the woman started up her car and drove off when Mr Johns appeared in the sitting-room behind her. 'I'm just off now,' he announced. 'I've got a couple more hours to do and that should finish it. All right with you if I come the same time tomorrow?'

Pernelle thought of her neighbour and his penchant for a lie-in on a Sunday morning. Her smile came out again. 'Perfectly all right,' she replied.

She did not see very much at all of her neighbour the next day. She guessed, when he left Myrtle Cottage early and did not return until late, that he had spotted Mr Johns' van draw up, and was not minded to have a second helping of yesterday's noise.

Momentarily she felt truly apologetic, because it couldn't be very pleasant for him to come to his weekend cottage, presumably for a little peace, and then have that peace shattered almost before he'd had time to garage his car. Still, it wouldn't be for much longer, she was just musing, when—good grief, what was she thinking of? Suddenly she woke up. He'd had a female visitor with him *all* day yesterday. True, she hadn't stayed as long this week as she had last week—by half an hour—but Pernelle would like to bet, Mr Johns or no Mr Johns, that nothing had been allowed to interfere with the 'peaceful' goings-on next door!

Eventually she dropped off to sleep, but was awakened at dawn on Monday by the sounds of her neighbour astir. It was still early when she heard his garage doors open and then the purr of his Jaguar.

Oddly, though, since she was certain she didn't give a button if she never saw him again, Pernelle could do nothing about the astounding urge that suddenly took charge of her and which decreed that she must see him.

Feeling totally unable to do anything but obey that compulsion, she got out of bed and—while being careful not to be seen should he inadvertently look up—stood behind the curtain and watched him go. And only then, when his Jaguar had disappeared from view, that compulsion to see him having been obeyed, did she pause to wonder at herself.

Good heavens, she thought shakenly, it was almost as if—as if—she couldn't bear for him to leave. As if—she didn't want him to go!

CHAPTER FOUR

BY LUNCHTIME that Monday, Pernelle had halfway convinced herself that the only reason she had shot out of bed to the window early that morning was to check on the weather. Any notion that she had been standing there watching Tremaine go because she wouldn't see him again until Friday, at the earliest, was totally ridiculous. As if she cared!

To show just how much she did not care, by Monday afternoon she had accepted a dinner date with Julian for Wednesday, and, despite starting to have doubts that she wanted to go out with Chris Farmer again, she had accepted a date with him for Saturday.

She returned home to Primrose Cottage on Monday evening, though with neither Tremaine, Julian, nor Chris Farmer in her head. Mike Yolland was on her mind all the way back to Chumleigh Edge. Mike was growing more despairing than ever, certain as he was that, given another year, he could be on top and all set for big success, but having huge problems in solving his immediate lack of working capital.

A problem of her own, with an electrical power point that night, put all men out of her head save Mr Eddie Johns. It was obvious she was going to have to call him back to the job. She rang him.

'Can't make it tomorrow,' he told her, sucking in his breath, 'I'm up to my eyes in it. Tell you what,' he offered after some seconds as Pernelle patiently waited to see what he could come up with, 'if I work through

lunch on Wednesday, I can get to your place about half
past four—how's that?'

'I'll leave a key under the dustbin,' she promptly accepted and, feeling suddenly guilty about his missed
lunch and aware of his coffee and tea-drinking abilities,
'Help yourself to tea or coffee,' she invited, then worked
with a will paperhanging.

Oddly, when she awoke on Tuesday, the man she
thought of on opening her eyes was Tremaine again! And
that made her cross. She once more most definitely
determined that she hated the loathsome man.

She went to work hating him, and indeed was hating
him so much that when just after eleven she answered
her phone and heard his voice, she thought for a moment
that the intensity of her feelings had caused her to hear
things.

'Who?' she demanded sharply.

'Hunter Tremaine,' he replied crisply, the voice undoubtedly his, even if his first name had until then been
unknown to her. 'Your neighbour,' he added, lest she
should still be in any doubt.

'What do you want?' she hurled at him aggressively.
And before he could begin to tell her, 'Look here, *you*,'
she hurried on explosively, 'it's enough that I've got you
living next door to me always complaining,' she exag-
gerated uncaringly, 'without you ringing me at work! I
think the best thing you can do is to...' Bluntly, he
chopped her off.

'I think the best thing you can do, Miss Richards, is
to hold it right there!'

'Don't you threaten me!' she erupted.

'I'll do what the hell I like, and you'll listen!' he rapped
curtly. And before she could throw the phone crashing

down to its rest, 'Unless, of course, you'd like me to report you to Yolland for insolence.'

'You...' she began to erupt again, but unexpectedly, some sixth sense seemed to be holding her back. 'What's my employer to do with you ringing me at work?' she challenged sharply instead.

'In point of fact, it's him I rang to have a word with,' he answered coolly.

'Why?' she questioned, that sixth sense working overtime.

'Not that I need to tell you my business, but, since you're Yolland's secretary, you'd be privy to it anyhow. I...'

'You're ringing Mr Yolland on a matter of business?' she queried, swallowing hard, and wanting to die at the way she'd spoken to Hunter Tremaine when it seemed likely that his firm might be putting some work their way. 'Er—what firm do you—er—represent?' she queried—and nearly had heart failure when he told her.

'Braddon Consolidated,' he replied crisply—and she almost fainted on the spot. She just did not want to believe that this man, Hunter Tremaine, who she'd just gone for hammer and tongs, appeared to be part of one of the biggest finance houses in the country—a finance house which Mike Yolland had written to asking them to back him. But Hunter Tremaine was ordering curtly, 'Put me through to your employer.'

'Yes, of course,' she answered, her secretarial self surfacing, even as she delayed to stammer, still not wanting to believe it, 'You w-work for Br-Braddon Consolidated?'

'I——' he paused, and then as if what he had said so far wasn't enough to make her horrified '—I happen to be its chairman,' he detailed.

Oh, please let this be a nightmare, a dream, Pernelle prayed as, her voice suddenly deserting her, she put the chairman of Braddon Consolidated through to Mike without another word.

But it wasn't a dream, she knew it wasn't, and even though there had been no way in which she could possibly have known who her neighbour was—or his connection with Braddons—until he told her, she had a dreadful feeling that she had just ruined things for Mike.

Oh, grief, Mike had been ready to grovel to anyone who'd step in and bail him out—and what had she done? 'What do you want?' she'd demanded—how was that for grovelling! 'Look here, *you*!' she'd gone on. Oh, lord, she couldn't bear to think about it!

Realising that she was shaking, although uncertain whether it was from crossing swords with Tremaine or the fact that she'd gone for his throat before she'd given him any chance to state his business, Pernelle took herself off to the cloakroom.

Ten minutes later she knew she could put off returning to her office no longer. She was certain by then, since Tremaine hadn't sounded in a giving mood, that he would have told Mike that there'd be no loan forthcoming.

She left the cloakroom knowing she would have to go and face Mike. Face him and confess that, when she could have been sweeter—heavens, what an understatement!—she had given the man he was most anxious should be afforded every courtesy nothing but all-out aggression.

Mike's office door was open when she went to her office, so she knew he had been in to see her. She was on the point of wondering if she should offer to resign when she realised he was on the phone to his wife, just finishing his call, in fact. Strangely, he was sounding remarkably cheerful!

Pernelle was standing by her desk when, his call over, he came through. He *was* cheerful, she realised, indeed, cock-a-hoop wasn't overstating it! 'You know who *that* was?' he grinned.

She didn't pretend to misunderstand him—she knew he was not referring to his wife. 'The man from Braddon Consolidated,' she replied, somehow finding she couldn't get the name Hunter Tremaine out.

'Only the chairman himself!' beamed Mike. 'I've just been talking to Zena. She, like me, reckons that Mr Tremaine, the chairman, wouldn't get involved unless they were seriously considering giving us a loan. Not that I'd have expected the chairman to take more than a fleeting interest in what can't seem very large by their standards, though it's a huge amount to me, but...'

'He's—they—Braddons, they're seriously considering offering a loan?' Pernelle interrupted him on a gasp.

'Fantastic, isn't it!' he agreed. 'Naturally my application will have to go in front of some sort of board along with everyone else's, but I don't doubt that Mr Tremaine will have the final say on whether I get it or not.'

'He told you you'd *got* the loan?' Pernelle asked in astonishment.

'If only it were that easy! No,' Mike told her, 'it'll probably take some time yet before I hear. What Mr Tremaine rang for was to put one or two pertinent questions. But he wouldn't do that if there wasn't any chance at all, would he? He said he'd be in touch again.'

Pernelle could only be glad for Mike, that after so many months of worry, weeks of going around in despair, and having heard from practically everybody but

Braddons—with a refusal—he should now start to look less despairing.

It was only after another evening of more decorating, when she was getting ready to go to bed, that it suddenly came to her that she hadn't breathed a word to Mike that Hunter Tremaine was—albeit only at weekends—her next-door neighbour.

She was still feeling fairly winded by the previous day's events when she got ready for work the next morning. Hunter Tremaine was much on her mind, and it was more by luck than anything else that at the last minute she remembered to tilt the dustbin to leave a key for the electrician.

She drove to work realising that a new element had entered her life, in that, while she would naturally be the epitome of a perfect secretary in her dealings with Hunter Tremaine at the office, just what did she do about Hunter Tremaine, her neighbour?

Without thinking about it, it wasn't very difficult to remember the times she had flared up at Tremaine—her neighbour. Would she be able to keep a check on her tongue should he do something this coming weekend to make her angry? Would he, in any case, expect her to stay meek, mild and all yes, sir, no, sir, three bags full, sir, in her own home? Somehow, though she couldn't have said why, she had a feeling he would not expect that at all.

Pernelle got on with her day knowing that while she most certainly would not be going all out looking for a fight—far from it—time alone would tell. Since, however, today was only Wednesday, she had two days at least in which to instil some sort of control in her recently—and strangely, only where he was concerned—awakened fiery temperament.

Her supposition that the earliest she would see Hunter Tremaine would be Friday proved wrong, however, when shortly after four that afternoon Reception rang to say that a Mr Tremaine was on his way up.

'Mr Tremaine?' Pernelle exclaimed, her blood suddenly starting to pulse a little faster through her veins. 'Mr Hunter Tremaine, do you mean?' she asked incredulously, even while she knew there just couldn't be two like him.

'I don't know his first name,' the receptionist replied anxiously. 'When I told him Mr Yolland was out, he asked where your office was, and though I knew I shouldn't—I don't know, there was just something about him—I heard myself smartly giving him directions. He was on his way by the time I'd recovered sufficiently to ask his fast-moving back for his name. "Tremaine", he tossed back at me in mid-stride.'

Pernelle had no trouble in imagining how it had been. Tall, confident and authoritative—the poor girl hadn't stood a chance. 'Don't worry about it, Karen,' she said lightly. 'Thanks for letting me know,' and she put the phone down.

A moment later she overcame the unexpected rush of emotion she experienced at the thought that Hunter Tremaine was on his way, and forced her secretarial brain into first gear. Mike had a busy afternoon engaged first with an appointment with his bank manager and, from there, he was going on to his accountant. According to how things went time-wise, he might or might not be back that afternoon, so he'd said.

Pernelle did a quick calculation and decided that, although both his appointments were important, that he should be here to see Hunter Tremaine was more important.

Swiftly she reached for the phone, but before she could so much as ask for an outside line her office door opened and Hunter Tremaine stepped in. Most oddly her heart gave a little flutter to see him, but she knew that was only because of the fact that he, being the chairman of Braddon Consolidated, could mean survival or extinction to Mike Yolland Plastics.

'Good afternoon, Mr Tremaine,' she smiled, aware that he'd know the receptionist had tipped her off about his arrival, and would not expect her to show surprise at seeing him. 'I'm afraid Mr Yolland's out just at the moment,' she brought her most efficient secretarial front to the fore.

He ignored her greeting. 'So I believe,' he stated coolly.

Pernelle had no intention of telling him where her employer was, but was fully aware of how vital it was to keep Hunter Tremaine sweet—though she doubted he was ever *that*. 'Would you like some refreshment?' she asked pleasantly, her mind racing to getting him sitting down—at her desk if need be—with a cup of tea, in the best china, of course, while she hared to a phone elsewhere in the building and told Mike to get back fast.

Hunter Tremaine declined her offer of refreshment purely by not referring to it. 'I'd like to take a look around,' he told her.

Great! The very chance she wanted. She smiled. By the sound of it, he really *was* considering putting some finance into the company! 'If you'd like to take a seat while I contact the works foreman, I...'

'We needn't take the foreman from his duties,' he cut her off, and had already turned back to the door when he decided, 'You can show me around.'

'Me?' Pernelle stopped him. He half turned, his all-seeing dark eyes flicking over her. 'But I don't know very much at all about...' Again she was interrupted.

'I'm sure you do,' he drawled, and had the door open while she was still trying to work out if his comment had been double-edged. In any event, it seemed that he was insisting that she show him around.

Because there was nothing else she could do if she was to keep him sweet, Pernelle closed her mind to the paperwork she had meant to complete before going home, and went with him. For courtesy's sake, though, if nothing else, she felt she just couldn't start walking around the factory area without at least introducing their visitor to the foreman.

'This is Dave Hickman, our foreman,' she introduced him, while looking hopefully for some sign that she had *imagined* that Hunter Tremaine was *insisting* she show him around, and that her presence was not after all required. But there was no such sign, so she completed the introductions. 'This is Mr Tremaine, who'd like to take a look over our plant and see what we do,' she said, and although Dave Hickman could have no idea what was going on she gave him top marks for understanding that it seemed important not to offend their guest.

'Shall we start over here?' he suggested, indicating a machine—which was a total mystery to Pernelle, and which stood near the entrance. She was still wondering if she could make her escape and get to a phone when to her chagrin, Hunter Tremaine firmly touched a hand to her elbow, indicating that she should follow. There was nothing for it, she had to accept, but to do the factory tour with them.

To her surprise, though, bearing in mind that Hunter Tremaine's field was finance, she discovered that he was most knowledgeable in other areas. He had a lightning grasp of anything Dave Hickman explained, and frequently came back with a pertinent question which, while she owned to being completely foxed, Dave heard and then went into more detailed explanation.

In no time at all Dave was looking at their visitor with a very genuine respect, and Pernelle was quickly realising that, when he wasn't being her unneighbourly neighbour, Hunter Tremaine was quite something else again.

They had nowhere near finished their tour, however, when at five to five, Pernelle glanced up and saw Mike Yolland, a flustered-looking Mike Yolland, hurrying in through the factory doors. Plainly Karen had told him that Mr Tremaine was here.

'Sorry I wasn't here when you arrived,' he apologised swiftly, even though he'd had no idea that Hunter Tremaine was expected. It was left to Pernelle to introduce them.

'Miss Richards and Mr Hickman here have been doing an excellent job in your absence,' Hunter Tremaine commented easily as the two shook hands.

'I'll take over if you like, Dave,' Mike told him when everyone started to pack up for the day.

Pernelle thought of the work waiting on her desk and wondered if *now* she could make her escape. But, as they moved on to the next machine, Hunter Tremaine again touched his hand to her elbow.

Eventually, when she saw from her watch that it was five past six, the tour of the plant was finished. Trying not to break out into a gallop, Pernelle strolled with them through the double doors. And, though she knew that all Mike wanted to talk about was work and the finance to back his particular work, she realised he was putting every effort into trying to hide how very much on thorns he was about the loan, by talking of everything and anything else.

Or was he? she wondered, as she heard him ask, 'Do you often come Wiltshire way?' and suddenly realised he was fishing to find out if Hunter Tremaine had come down especially to see him and his factory—in which case, all the signs would look fair.

'I manage to get down most weekends,' Hunter answered, going on—when Pernelle hadn't found time yet to tell Mike who her neighbour was— 'I've a small cottage in Chumleigh Edge.'

'Chumleigh Edge?' Mike exclaimed, startled, and while Pernelle could do nothing but stand there and feel guilty about her omission, 'That's where Pernelle lives!'

'So she does,' Hunter Tremaine agreed, and added, 'We're—neighbours.'

'Neighbours? But her neighbour is . . .'

'Would you excuse me?' Pernelle butted in quickly before Mike could tell him any of the isolated but nonetheless derogatory statements she had made about her neighbour. She smiled generally and, her composure starting to fracture, turned from them and made smart tracks for her office.

She still hadn't got herself very much together some five minutes later, though she was blessed if she could figure out why she should suddenly feel so flustered. But, glancing down at her desk, she saw that she just couldn't put her work in her drawer and forget about it until the morning.

But working late had never bothered her, though first of all, knowing that the receptionist would have switched a line through, she picked up her phone. With luck Julian should have arrived home from his office by now.

She had dialled his home number, and he had just answered, when Mike *and* Hunter Tremaine came in. For a split second Pernelle hovered between replacing the receiver, to make her call later, or getting on with it now.

It was the obstinate thought that she didn't believe for a moment that Hunter Tremaine could possibly be the cause for her going to pieces not so long back that decided her to carry on with her call. 'Hello, Julian. It's Pernelle.' She gave her attention to the phone, and while Mike went poking around in one of her cabinets, she transferred her gaze to Hunter as she told Julian, 'Sorry to leave it so late, but can I cry off our date tonight?'

Julian, super person that she knew him to be, seemed in turn to know she wouldn't cancel their arrangement needlessly, and did not argue the case. 'How about tomorrow?' he suggested. 'I'm free if you are.'

She was just about to reply when it suddenly struck her that Hunter Tremaine, clearly tuned into what she had been saying, was looking more pleased than she had ever seen him! He was more than sharp enough to have realised that she had cancelled her date because, through him and his unexpected arrival—and his insistence that she tour the factory with him—she was running late. But was he looking regretful on hearing her having to cancel her arrangements? Was he hell! He was positively smirking!

'Tomorrow night's out?' Julian guessed when the seconds had ticked by and she hadn't answered.

'Tomorrow night will be fine,' she replied swiftly, saw Hunter Tremaine frown, then looked away from him while she quickly completed her call, then went to help Mike, who was plainly having no luck in finding whatever it was he was looking for.

'Ah, Pernelle,' he said in relief. 'That literature we had printed on the new and exciting innovation we've got all lined up. I thought Mr Tremaine might like to see a copy, but...'

In seconds Pernelle had efficiently found what Mike had been looking for, and had handed a copy over to their visitor. He did not read it there and then—she had hardly expected him to.

Seconds later he was shaking hands with her employer prior to leaving. All she got was a curt nod. Grateful for small offerings, she got on with some work when Mike suddenly decided to go down to Hunter Tremaine's car with him.

He was soon back, however, and, as Pernelle had anticipated, more than a little curious that she'd said nothing to him about the chairman of Braddons being her weekend neighbour.

'So why the secrecy about the occupant of Myrtle Cottage?' was his first question.

'I honestly didn't know who he was, Mike,' she replied. 'Not until yesterday, when he rang to speak to you, did I even know what work he did, much less that he as good as runs Braddon Consolidated. I just never associated the man who bossily suggested I get busy in my garden...' She broke off when she could see from Mike's expression that, of course, he believed her.

Though she wasn't sure she could handle his, 'Well, you won't be having any sharp words with him in future, I hope!'

In the light of Mike's nervousness that the least thing might cause Hunter Tremaine to give the thumbs down on the loan, all Pernelle could do was to smile and hope that conveyed that she would do her best. Then swiftly she changed tack. 'I couldn't get free to phone to let you know that he was here, but I was so glad you came back instead of going straight home.'

'So am I!' he said fervently, adding, 'I nearly collapsed when I asked Karen who owned the Jag parked outside and she told me a Mr Tremaine!'

Pernelle cleared her desk at a few minutes before seven and went home. There was no sign of the Jaguar on her neighbour's path, but as she entered Primrose Cottage and set about making herself a snack, sounds from Myrtle Cottage muffled their way through, and, oddly, she could not prevent a small smile.

She rejected entirely any ridiculous notion that she might—what a hoot!—be pleased that he was in residence. Quite obviously his car was garaged. She turned her mind to other matters, and made herself a pot of tea.

If she wanted a reminder, however, that Mr Johns had been due to fix her power point that afternoon, she discovered that he had in fact been when she went to get the milk out of the fridge. Of milk there was none. Clearly, her invitation to 'help yourself to tea or coffee' had been taken as 'or a pint of milk if you fancy one'.

By then Pernelle realised that she was gasping for a cup of tea. Another small sound from next door again brought her neighbour to mind. She hurriedly chased him out again. They were just not the sort of neighbours that she could nip round next door to borrow some milk from. Anyhow, the milkman came at about six in the morning—she'd manage without milk until then.

She spent the rest of the evening putting the finishing touches to her bedroom and moving back in. Then, it having been a wearying day one way or another, she was glad to fall into bed.

She slept soundly in her newly decorated bedroom, but was awake early. Her first action on getting out of bed was to open her bedroom windows and peer down to the gravel path directly in front of the two cottages. Good, the milkman had been.

It was drizzling with rain, but the atmosphere was warm and sticky, so she left the bedroom window ajar on the first latch for a little air, and dived downstairs to put the kettle to boil.

Her sights were set solely on the lovely cup of tea she would have when, clad in her short nightshirt—it was too stickily close to bother with a dressing-gown—she popped her head out prior to picking up her bottle of milk.

Her troubles began in that the milkman had, for some reasons best known to himself, placed her milk a yard or two further away from her door than was normal. A quick glance around showed that no one was about. Which caused her to be in no particular hurry as she stepped through her front door and over to pick up her milk and also a leaflet the milkman had left. She took a brief scan of the leaflet, noted that there was a special price on orange juice from next Monday, and turned round—to gasp, to rush, and to get her extended left hand to her front door, just as it slammed shut.

Open-mouthed, disbelieving, she stared at the door in alarm as it quickly dawned on her that she was locked out! For a moment, as she stood in the drizzling rain clutching on to a bottle of milk and a leaflet, her brain seized up. Then, while she was cursing her efficient self that she had remembered to collect her spare rear door key from beneath the dustbin where Mr Johns had returned it, her brain began to function again.

Her first acknowledgement was that she was in a fair pickle. Her second that she couldn't stand there clutching a bottle of milk all day. She put the milk down, and the leaflet, and concentrated her thoughts on gaining entry to her property.

All the downstairs windows were securely fastened, she knew that without checking. She looked up at her bedroom window. A ladder—what she needed was a ladder. Suddenly she felt sure she'd glimpsed a ladder in Hunter Tremaine's garage one time.

Hastily, and as silently as she could, she picked her lightly slippered feet over the gravel, passed through the gap between wall and hedge where their two properties divided, and hurried through and on to his garage. Unfairly, she hated him some more for being no less efficient than she, in that his garage was locked.

Damn him! she fumed, and came close to kicking his garage doors. By the time she'd got herself back on her own side of the gravel, though, she was wondering at the unfairness of her thoughts, when she had always been so fair-minded. Most peculiarly, her emotions seemed to start to get churned up when Hunter Tremaine, or thoughts of him, began to get to her.

She dismissed him from her mind, then changed her mind about its being a warm and sticky day. Her nightshirt was beginning to cling wetly to her, and she was feeling far from comfortable.

However, none of that was solving her problem. Trust Tremaine to be a lie-a-bed! She glared up at his bedroom window. If he was any use he'd be up and coming to her aid. It... She chopped her thoughts off—there she was, being unfair again. Hunter Tremaine hadn't got where he was without working darned hard for it, had he? He'd earned the chance of a lie-in now and then.

She was, in some surprise, beginning to wonder when she had switched from hating the brute to wanting to give him a fair hearing, when she realised that it was still quite early anyhow.

Even so, she couldn't stand out here for much longer—she was becoming more soaked by the minute. She flicked another glance up at Hunter Tremaine's bedroom window. At least, since he had two bedrooms, she assumed that he was using the larger of the two.

She was loath to disturb him, but he did have a ladder, she was growing convinced of that—and the alternative was for her to trudge, in her sopping wet nightshirt, half a mile to the village and throw herself on the mercy of the village policeman.

Her mind made up for her when it suddenly began to rain more heavily, she opened her mouth to call Tremaine's name, when she suddenly remembered his Saturday female visitor. Oh, dear—what if he was 'entertaining'?

More rain plastered her hair wetly to her head, and— oh, to hell with it, what if he was? 'Tre... Mr Tremaine!' she called. No answer. *'Mr Tremaine!'* she called again, and waited. *'Mr Tremaine—Hunter!'* she yelled, and was hating him afresh that when he slept, he slept the sleep of the dead.

Exasperatedly, she looked down to her sodden slipper-clad feet, but saw not her feet, but the gravel—loads of it.

Her first piece of gravel thrown up at his window drew no response, as with her second, third, fourth and fifth. Damn him, damn him to hell, she thought crossly, and found a much larger piece of gravel—not to say a small rock—and in damp, cross desperation, she hurled that

up at his bedroom window. It landed exactly on target—
and *crack* went the window.

Horror-struck, Pernelle was still staring disbelievingly
at her handiwork when Hunter Tremaine appeared and
opened his window. He was bare-chested, his damp hair
denoting that he'd just come from the shower. She
guessed he'd that moment entered his bedroom just as
she'd cracked his window. He was not best pleased!

She could tell that as she raised her eyes from his broad
hair-roughened chest and met his steely glance full on.
'Break it, why don't you?' he snarled.

'I've locked myself out,' she replied by way of
explanation.

He flicked his gaze over her thin and by then trans-
parent-where-it-touched cotton nightshirt. 'Tough!' he
rapped, and as she folded her arms in front of her, he
slammed the window shut. The glass fell out.

Pernelle was glad, glad, glad. She hoped it blew a gale
all day and that his bedroom got as soaked as she was.
The swine, the unhelpful pig! she raged silently, and
railed against him for another few minutes before a
feeling of utter dejection started to set in. What on earth
was she going to do now?

She was still pondering that question when simul-
taneously, as if the gods would have it no other way, the
rain suddenly stopped and, business-suited and briefcase
in hand, Hunter Tremaine came out.

By then Pernelle was ready to beg him for assistance,
but, as he flicked a glance at her before going to his
garage and unlocking it, 'I'll pay for the window,' was
the furthest she found she could go.

'Too true!' he retorted, and unlocked his garage doors.

She listened for the sound of his car purring into life,
but heard no such sound. And when, a few minutes later,

she saw not a car emerge from the garage, but one end of a ladder, she was ready to take back every one of the uncomplimentary things she had ever thought or said about him.

She was not so sure about that, though, when, having disposed of his suit jacket, and having walked past her without a word and placed the ladder up against her bedroom window, Hunter Tremaine stood back and extended a hand in invitation that she should shin up the ladder.

'Oh, come *on*!' she appealed, having enough to contend with in her above-the-knee, now almost transparent nightshirt without having to climb up a ladder while he stood at the bottom of it.

Unexpectedly, then, she could have sworn there was a definite twinkle of devilment in his eyes, and that he was only teasing. But the sound of a motor vehicle suddenly penetrated, and Pernelle was suddenly far more concerned with finding a hiding place than in double-checking to see what look Hunter Tremaine wore in his eyes.

Without a please or thank you she grabbed hold of him and hid herself behind him, peeping out just as the parcel post van went by the two cottages.

'You modest little soul!' Hunter Tremaine taunted, but, to her utmost relief, he started up the ladder and in no time had disappeared through her bedroom window.

Any idea she might have gleaned that he was all at once in a surprisingly good humour swiftly evaporated when he opened her front door and let her in. They were both standing in her newly decorated sitting-room, Hunter Tremaine blocking her way so that she couldn't get past him to her kitchen and thereby her stairs when, before she could open her mouth to thank him for helping her out, he instructed her shortly, 'You'd better hang about until Mrs Moore can get here!'

'You're expecting her this morning?' Pernelle questioned coolly—in her view he was too bossy by half.

'I'll ring her when I ring the glazier. If she can't make it, you'll have to wait here yourself until the glazier turns up.'

'Anything else?'

He looked her over coolly, obviously not thrilled by her uppity attitude. '*You* broke the bloody window, not me!' he reminded her grittily.

'What's it like to be perfect?' she asked, nettled.

'*You'll* never know!' he flung at her, and, for no reason she could understand, his reply made her lips twitch. What was more, when, not wanting him to see that he had somehow touched to her sense of humour, she went to push past him, she suddenly hit the rock wall of his body, and looked up. Unbelievably, his lips were twitching too. Dark blue eyes were all at once burning into melting brown eyes, and as he growled something that sounded very much like, 'You're incorrigible, Miss Richards,' he gathered her into his arms.

Pernelle was never certain how it happened that without a murmur of protest she was suddenly in his arms, but, having found herself there, she felt no great urgency to be free. The reason for that, she soon realised as his head came down and his mouth met hers, was that never had she been kissed quite like it. His kiss, his touch, all at once made her want to give and give. She clung mindlessly to him, loving the feel of his warmth. His kiss was commanding, yet giving too, and was wonderful. The strength of his manly arms about her was thrilling, and she yielded her body up to him.

Yet, while she was aware of a great tide of passion growing and flowing between them, it was Hunter Tremaine who broke that kiss and, staring down into her flushed face, put some daylight between their two bodies.

Feeling mesmerised, Pernelle stared back, totally oblivious of her soggy night attire, or the fact that some of her dampness must be transferring itself to him. Reality, in fact, only returned when, touching a hand to her wet shoulder he ordered, 'Go and take a hot shower.'

Pernelle stepped shakenly back a step and out of his arms. 'Perhaps you should go and take a cold one,' she retorted, even while she was amazed that her voice should come out sounding so husky, fully aware that the passion in that kiss had by no means been all one-sided.

Hunter's eyes flicked down to her parted lips, then down to where her breasts were firmly pushing at the damp cotton that covered her. She saw a muscle jerk in his temple. 'Perhaps—I should—stay,' he suggested, his voice all at once slightly gravelly.

But, as his hands came to her waist and he began to draw her close again, she felt suddenly panicky.

'G-goodbye,' she said chokily—and then the oddest thing yet happened. For although Hunter must have known she would not have put up much resistance with the two of them alone, she suddenly felt churned up inside—and *affectionate* towards him—when, letting his hands fall to his sides, he marvellously, and un-expectedly, grinned, and backed off.

'Perhaps you're right,' he murmured, and abruptly left her.

Pernelle was still feeling stunned by her feelings, his feelings, *that grin*, when she heard the Jaguar purr down

the drive. Had that been he, the Hunter Tremaine she
knew, who had taken her in his arms and had so warmly,
so giving, so commandingly kissed her? Heaven help
her—he was dynamite!

CHAPTER FIVE

TWENTY-FOUR hours later Pernelle was still trying to get over the dynamism of her neighbour. Though, if she was still staggered by him, she was absolutely amazed by her own fevered response to just *one kiss*. What in creation had got into her?

She went home from work that evening not yet recovered from her shaken feeling that, when she knew she was just not the type of person to be so unrestrained with anyone and never had been, 'unrestrained' just about covered her behaviour.

It was solely because of that, of course, she realised, that she seemed unable to get Hunter out of her head. Not that she'd stood much chance of pushing him to the back of her mind anyhow, not with Mike, both yesterday and today, making some reference to him.

'Naturally Mr Tremaine will want to discuss any loan he's considering with his board,' he'd told her yesterday morning. 'I hope Braddon Consolidated have a board meeting weekly, rather than monthly,' he'd muttered anxiously yesterday afternoon. And today, clearly no less worried than he had been, 'I expect you'll be seeing Mr Tremaine this weekend when he comes down?' Mike had suggested, and gave Pernelle a little something else to think about.

'He doesn't always come down,' she replied, and, while her heart went out to Mike and the strain he was under, she hoped he was not also suggesting what it very much sounded as though he *was* suggesting. For, with a sinking feeling, it sounded to her ears just as though he wanted her to ask Hunter Tremaine when she saw him just how his loan application was going!

She made herself a sketchy meal that Friday evening, and, while she completed the painting of the woodwork in the bathroom, she worried that, though she wanted to do everything she could do to help Mike, she felt she could not do what he wanted with regard to Hunter. Mike knew in any case, from the occasional snippet she'd shared, that she and Hunter were not good neighbours. Surely, when he thought about it, Mike must see anyhow that she and the chairman of Braddons were not so well acquainted that she could put any such enquiry to him.

Pernelle then remembered how, clad in next to nothing, she had been warmly enfolded in Hunter's arms only yesterday morning. Not so well acquainted! 'Oh, grief!' she groaned, and was back on a treadmill of wondering what had got into her yesterday.

There seemed no escape from the man; when, quite late, she fell into bed, he was still there in her head. She ousted him by deliberately switching her thoughts to Julian, dear uncomplicated Julian with whom she'd had dinner last night. Then she discovered that Hunter was back in her head again when she found she was reflecting that to have a cottage in this part of the world where he could come each weekend must mean that Hunter had bought Myrtle Cottage as a place to 'get away from it all'. A place where he certainly wouldn't want to be reminded of work—which was what she feared Mike wanted her to do.

Again she ousted Hunter, to go over again how she had yesterday morning waited for Mrs Moore, who in turn—while attending to a few chores inside Myrtle Cottage—had waited for the glazier. When she'd returned home last night from Mike Yolland Plastics, the window pane had been replaced and everything looked back to normal.

But everything was not back to normal. For Hunter was suddenly back in her head once more when she discovered she was listening for the sound of his car. For goodness' sake, what was the matter with her! As if she cared a button that, because he'd come to Myrtle Cottage mid-week, he might have decided not to come down this weekend!

Pernelle determined that she was not listening for the sounds of his car, and pulled the covers up over her head and tried to sleep. Curiously though, when she had never before had any problems in sleeping, she could not get off to sleep that night. In fact, not until somewhere around four o'clock on Saturday morning when, with dawn breaking, she heard the purr of a Jaguar and then the click of a gate, did she settle down to some sound sleep.

She was up early and had awakened in a contented frame of mind. The only room in her cottage that had not been fully decorated was her bathroom. Luckily the previous owner had installed a modern bathroom unit, so, having already prepared the walls, all she had to do was apply a couple of coats of emulsion.

At a few minutes before midday Pernelle stepped back to survey her handiwork and decided that a break wouldn't come amiss. All was quiet next door when, for no special reason, she ambled into her bedroom and took a look out of the front window.

A minute after that, a smart car drove up, slowed, and was parked. When a smartly dressed woman stepped out and hurried up the drive of Myrtle Cottage, Pernelle's brow wrinkled and, most peculiarly, all at once she found she was not feeling as contented as she had been. She stood for quite some time admiring her view, but, quite plainly, the woman was no casual caller, for she did not reappear.

Indeed, not until about ten to four, when Pernelle again happened to be admiring the view from her bedroom window, did she see the woman leave.

Womanising swine! she fumed, and went downstairs, wrote herself a small shopping list and, at a brisk pace, went for a walk to the village.

She had just been served a lettuce and a few other oddments when the woman assistant, halfway through giving her her change, clearly suddenly found a fresh customer entering the shop of much more interest. Pernelle was in the act of following the direction of the assistant's beaming gaze when the woman said warmly, 'Good afternoon, Mr Tremaine.'

My stars, Pernelle fumed, no woman was safe from him! Stuffing her change into her purse she did a sharp about-turn—and cursed fate that her eyes met his directly. But, just as it looked as though he might acknowledge her, she stuck her head in the air and sailed out of the shop.

In the half-mile walk home Pernelle had plenty of time in which to want that moment back. She had handled it all wrong, of course. What she should have done was to... When she reached Primrose Cottage she was wishing with all she had that she had never gone up to the village store. She was going out to dinner that night, so she hadn't needed anything so vitally.

Half an hour later she was seated in her sitting-room with a cup of tea when the sound of Hunter Tremaine furiously thumping on the wall that divided them made her jump in alarm.

'What the...?' she cried out loud, but, having shot to her feet, she was able to see from her window 'what the...' Seven or eight sheep had made their way from common land into her garden and, obviously finding her garden boring, were crossing—indeed, some *had* crossed—into Hunter's garden, and were delightedly feasting on the glorious blooms which his gardener tended weekly.

Oh, help, Pernelle thought, and with nothing in her garden that could come to very much harm, she raced outside to shoo the sheep away lest they ate some flower which might prove poisonous to them.

Hunter had come out too, she observed, and discovered that the word 'shoo' meant nothing to them and that the sheep she was trying to turn had just gone through the gap in front of the two cottages.

'Haven't you any sense?' Hunter Tremaine blasted her eardrums.

The nerve! 'How can I have when you've got it all?' she flared.

'I've got enough to know that when you live in the country—or anywhere else, for that matter—you don't go around leaving gates open!' he lobbed back at her before she could blink.

'My gates are...' She broke off as she looked down to where her gates should have been closed. Where she was certain she had closed them when she'd come in, one of the pair was now wide open. 'I'm sure I...' she began again, but he had moved away and was chivvying the sheep down his drive and out through gates which he had just opened.

It seemed an age later when, by dint of clapping her hands behind them, she had rounded up 'her sheep' and driven them out through her gates—from where they would again soon come to some common land.

She was not ecstatic that Hunter Tremaine stood there watching her performance. Though since, if she didn't get them all out, they would only go back and eat his borders again, she could hardly blame him. But blame him she did that, having closed the gates on the last of her visitors, he was still there watching her as she walked back up the drive.

She had, she remembered without the smallest difficulty, stuck her nose in the air and walked past him in the village shop—and had very soon regretted it. She drew level with him; he was still watching her. She would not walk past him this time without a word, to again regret it the minute he was out of sight.

Hostilely she glanced across at him, and there was no thought whatsoever in her head then of Mike, and how he wanted her to be nice to her neighbour, when she opened her mouth and told him waspishly, 'I hope your clematis dies!'

She had taken a step to her front door when she heard him laugh. Damn him, she had amused him! She took another step to her front door when she saw that it had again slammed shut behind her—in her haste to get to the sheep, she hadn't thought to prop it open. Pernelle veered from her path and carried on walking down the side of her cottage where Hunter could not see her. She had a vague recollection that she had left her back door unlocked, but if she hadn't, she'd camp out rather than ask for his assistance again.

To her relief her back door *was* unlocked, but her neighbour was very much on her mind when, forgetful that she had a cup of tea going cold in her sitting-room, she went upstairs to take a bath.

Pernelle owned, as she waited for Chris Farmer to call for her that evening, that her heart was not really in this date. In fact, had Chris phoned at the last minute to say that he couldn't make it, she would have been more pleased than annoyed.

But he did not ring, but arrived five minutes before time. Attired in an amber-coloured dress that did justice to her shape, Pernelle clicked her front door locked behind her and went down her drive to greet her date.

'Hello, Chris,' she smiled. 'How are you?'

'Better for seeing you,' he replied, and she discovered she didn't want to go out with him at all.

But, because she *had* agreed to go out with him, she got into his car and did her best to enjoy the evening. But it was all wrong, and she knew this was the last date she'd be having with Chris Farmer long before the evening was over—and that made her feel guilty.

It was that guilt, guilt that, having accepted his invitation out, she might not have come across as a very enthusiastic dinner partner, that made her attempt to redress the balance when he drove her home.

'Do I get to come in for a coffee tonight?' he asked as he pulled up outside her home.

A cup of coffee wouldn't hurt you, the voice of guilt nagged her. 'Of course,' she smiled. 'You can come in and have a look at my redecorating now that it's finished.'

Inside her cottage, Pernelle left him in her sitting-room while she went to make some coffee. With Julian on Thursday she had taken him upstairs to show off her newly decorated bedroom, but Julian was a friend, a good friend, and would never have dreamt of taking advantage of being in her bedroom. With Chris Farmer, she didn't have that confidence.

Suddenly Chris was joining her in the kitchen. 'I got lonely in there on my own,' he said suggestively, and as he came over to her and put his arms round her, Pernelle knew she had been right not to take him upstairs to admire her paper-hanging ability.

'Coffee *only*, Chris,' she told him lightly as she attempted to back out of his arms.

'You're joking,' he smirked, and to her annoyance, tried to pull her closer.

'I am *not* joking,' she told him shortly.

'Sure you are.' He refused to believe her. 'Strewth, we've been out three times now! You've got to be joking if you think I'm going home empty-handed tonight!'

Pernelle didn't like the sound of this, not one little bit. 'I think you'd better go now, without waiting for coffee,' she told him stiffly, and, intending to get through to the sitting-room and open the front door, she pushed him away.

She'd barely taken a step towards her sitting-room, though, when he grabbed her from behind and pushed her up against a wall. Oh, heavens, she thought shakily, when she saw a look of pure lust in his face. Desperately she strove to stay calm.

'Take your hands off me, and go!' she ordered him, her voice, despite her fight for control, starting to rise.

'Not before I've had what you've been teasing me with all night,' he leered, and dragged her roughly to him.

A scream escaped her, then she had no breath for anything but to fight him off. Although that fight didn't last very long, for, while she was oblivious to what sort of commotion she was creating, suddenly, to her great joy, the outside door into her kitchen was flung open, and Hunter Tremaine was there.

'Hunter!' she cried, such was her relief that she barely knew she had called him by his first name.

He looked absolutely enraged, she saw, as he glared over to where Chris still had his arms about her. But she didn't care how enraged Hunter looked—he was here, and that was all that mattered. By some miracle, he was here, and Chris, plainly thwarted at the arrival of a third party, soon had his ardour cooled.

He attempted to argue, however—if not for long— when from his superior height Hunter, his rage under control, looked down at him and clipped, 'You heard the lady. Take your hands off her, and go.'

'And if I don't?'

Hunter surveyed him as if he were a maggot, then shrugged as though he found him extremely tedious. 'So we'll do it the hard way,' he muttered, and took a menacing step towards him.

'There's no need for any rough stuff.' Chris folded instantly and, letting her go, backed away, and with Hunter following him he did a quick exit out through the sitting-room, and through the front door, and down the drive.

Feeling extremely shaken, Pernelle stood rooted, but was honestly certain that in her efforts to seem pleased to be out with her date she could not have given him the 'teasing' impression he had suggested.

She still hadn't moved from where she had been standing when she heard the sound of Chris's car engine fade away, and, as it crossed her mind that Hunter might be so angry at being disturbed that he would go to his own cottage without bothering to return, she heard the slam of her front door.

Then Hunter was coming back to her kitchen, was favouring her with a hard, cursory glance, and then, without a word, was striding over to the other outer door. His right hand was on the door handle when Pernelle's gratitude to him overflowed. 'Th-thank you,' she told him huskily.

He turned, his angry dark eyes going over her pale face and huge-eyed, shaken appearance. He gave her a curt nod, but when it seemed he would go, he hesitated, and suddenly some of his aggression seemed to leave him.

'Are you all right?' he questioned gruffly, and took a step towards her.

'F-fine,' she lied, feeling close to tears but striving with all she had not to break down.

Again Hunter studied her face, her wide brown eyes that were shining with tears she refused to shed, and which looked more melting than ever. And unexpectedly, his expression softened. 'Oh—come here,' he grunted, and the next she knew, he had moved nearer, had reached for her, and gently enfolded her in his arms.

For perhaps one second, maybe two, Pernelle stood rigid in his hold. But he made no attempt to kiss her, but just cradled her to him—and all at once some great tension went out of her, and she collapsed against him.

Minutes ticked by as Pernelle acknowledged that when finding herself in Chris Farmer's arms had caused her alarm, Hunter's arms, by contrast, seemed a haven. Gradually, however, she started to get herself back together again, and she stirred in his gentle hold—then wished she hadn't when, although unhurriedly, those arms that had given her such comfort suddenly fell away.

Hunter took a couple of steps back and looked into her face as though to gauge for himself how she was feeling. Bravely, grateful to him, grateful that her feeling of wanting to burst into tears had gone, she stared back at him—and loved the quirky grin that came to his face as he queried, 'Thinking of seeing him again?'

Pernelle laughed—she couldn't help it. But, as a thought suddenly struck her, 'How did you get in?' she asked.

'Your door was unlocked,' he replied.

'Really!' she exclaimed, though she had no memory of actually checking to see if she'd turned the old-fashioned key in the lock before she'd gone out through the other door.

'Would I lie?' he asked lightly, and she smiled.

'I don't think you would.'

'You all right now?' he queried seriously.

'Fine,' she replied, and this time meant it.

'So, goodnight, fair maid,' he murmured, and, taking hold of her right hand, he raised it to his lips, kissed it, and left her, and Pernelle floated up to bed. Somehow she had received a definite impression that had Hunter been unable to get in, he would have broken the door down to rescue her.

It gave her a very nice feeling. One way and another, she decided, she had, after all, a very good neighbour.

Not very many hours later, however, she was re-thinking any such pleasant thoughts about her good neighbour. She had, with an idea that had awakened with her on Sunday morning, decided she would be a good neighbour too. Having taken on board his objection to wandering livestock chewing up his flower beds, she thought she would do something about it. While that gap between the front dividing hedge and the front wall of the two cottages was still there, there was always going to be a possibility of unwanted visitors on her property taking a stroll on to his.

At a little after nine, armed with some twine and some old pieces of wood she found on a shelf in the shed, she set about erecting a fence between the two cottages.

Half an hour later she had completed her task, and although it looked a bit of a hotch-potch effort, she had to own, she couldn't see any wayward sheep getting by it and through to next door. Not unless, she suddenly realised, they could jump a two-foot hedge.

She had just gone into the realms of wondering how high, when determined, sheep could jump, when suddenly her neighbour came round the side of his property, looked her way, and stopped dead.

A sudden and most inexplicable feeling of shyness washed over Pernelle, and as Hunter stepped on to the front path and started to come over, she looked down while she pulled herself together.

She had barely started on a self-lecture that began—twenty-two and suddenly suffering from shyness, for goodness' sake!—than Hunter demanded, 'What in the devil's name do you call *that*?' his harsh accusatory tone causing her to raise her head swiftly in astonishment.

Gone, she saw at once, was the kind neighbour who had rescued her last night, who had given her a gentle cuddle until she was over a very unpleasant experience and had then, like a knight of old, kissed her hand and gone. Here, staring antagonistically at her handiwork, was the man she was more used to seeing.

'You objected to having sheep in your garden yesterday!' she retorted sharply, her shyness sent flying at his aggressive tone. 'I thought I'd keep them out with a fence.'

'You could keep them out by remembering to shut your gates!' he hurled back at her, and before she could rise to that, he prodded the wood and twine fence and told her in no uncertain terms, 'It looks a mess! I'm not having it on my property!'

'It isn't on your property!' she argued hotly.

'That string's attached to my down-pipe!' he rapped.

Actually, Pernelle had no idea who owned the down-pipe. But, 'Right!' she snapped. 'But just be sure you keep your gates closed too. It works both ways, you know.'

'Huh!' he scorned, and Pernelle was hating him again to think that while she was bending over trying to undo knots which she'd tied so fast that they were never meant to be undone, he just stood there and watched.

She was hating him with a vengeance when she broke a nail and still couldn't get one particularly stubborn knot undone. And there was no lessening in her hatred of him when he went off somewhere, for he was not away long, before he returned—with a pair of scissors.

In silence they both dismantled the rest of the make-do fence. They straightened at the same time, she to glare up at him, ready for war, he to stare down at her in a superior manner, not one whit bothered.

Though, as she went to turn away without another word, she was suddenly surprised into stillness when, quite unexpectedly, he questioned, 'You were genuinely scared last night, weren't you?'

Pernelle looked at him, and the fact of his statement, that when he'd just been such a brute he could still be the same man who'd shown such gentleness to her last night, caused her to answer, quite idiotically, she at once realised, 'Of you, do you mean?'

'Not me, clown!' Hunter answered shirtily. 'Him—your date!'

'Thanks!' she snapped, not thrilled to be called a clown, even if she had owned that her reply had been idiotic. Though since she'd got no intention of repeating to the brute how Chris Farmer had seemed to believe she had been leading him on all evening, and since Hunter Tremaine seemed to be waiting for an answer— though why she should feel she had to answer him, she didn't know, 'I—er—got in a little over my head, I suppose,' she answered, and realised then that since Hunter had come and rescued her, perhaps she owed him that much.

She thought, though, that Hunter looked slightly taken aback as he digested what she had just said. He stared at her for some long silent seconds anyhow before, slowly, he at last enquired, 'You're not a virgin, though?'

Honestly! Was there no end to his nerve? 'Why *not*?' Pernelle challenged shortly, and had some quite un-required expletive hit her ears. 'Thanks,' she snapped again.

'Thanks be damned,' he snarled. 'You want your head examined!'

'Why?' she wanted to know—because she was a virgin and shouldn't be? she wondered.

'Because anyone could see the type of man he is!' Hunter Tremaine roared.

'Well, *you'd* know!' she snapped, and could see that he didn't look too enchanted that she had just more or less stated that he'd know because he was the same type. And that, she swiftly realised when she recalled how Hunter had cradled her to him and had gently cuddled her until she felt much less shaky, was most unfair. 'Anyhow,' she somehow felt obliged to add more pleasantly, 'I only wanted to show off my home, the decorating I'd done, and he...'

It was nearest she could come to an apology in the circumstance of Hunter being the brute he was this morning. But it was plain that he wasn't interested in an apology, whatever form it took. For, 'Huh!' he scorned halfway through what she was saying, and strode off to his garage.

Pig! she fumed and, gathering up wood and twine, went and dumped the lot unceremoniously in her shed and went indoors.

She spent most of that day gardening out at the back if Hunter was in the front, and when he came round that way she went indoors to telephone her mother.

'When are you coming to see us?' her mother wanted to know. Since Bruce no longer had business in the Wiltshire area, the frequency of their visits was becoming less and less.

'When I've got my garden in some sort of shape,' Pernelle replied, and a little later came off the phone to observe that Hunter was doing something out in his back garden. Taking care to fasten the latch back on her front door, she found plenty to do in her front garden.

She later went indoors, pleased with her achievement. So OK, her garden was a long way from being the picture her next-door neighbour's garden was but, now that her redecorating was out of the way, she'd have far more spare time. Perhaps she'd buy some plants to put in tomorrow, she mused as she went upstairs to wash her hair and take a bath.

After her bath she donned clean jeans and a fresh white shirt, then went downstairs, made herself a meal and, for no reason she could think of, found she was wondering what her neighbour was doing for a meal.

A second later she was scorning the thought that she was in any way whatsoever the least bit interested in how Hunter Tremaine filled his arrogant, swinish frame.

She was in her kitchen drying up the last utensils after her meal, however, when she heard his back door being closed. A second later she heard his feet scrunching over the gravel—coming in her direction!

Most ridiculously her heart suddenly set up a crazy beat, and she hastily turned her back to the kitchen window to put the fork in her hand in the cutlery drawer. Then a knock sounded at her kitchen door. Somehow, it sounded a friendly knock, but she'd been fooled by signs of friendship from Hunter before, so she went to answer it all ready to shoot him down in flames before he opened his mouth.

She was totally unprepared, though, for the fact that while leaning on the doorframe with one hand, Hunter should be holding a bottle of wine in the other. It rendered her speechless, and allowed him to get in first as he queried, with one eyebrow going off at a quirky angle, 'Want to show me your decorating?'

Her mouth fell a little way open. The last time she'd seen him to speak to they'd been snarling at each other! Yet here he was, if she was not mistaken, actually *teasing* her! She felt a joyous laugh begin somewhere deep within her, and, although she was determined to hold that unfathomable laugh down, such was the effect of his affable teasing of her that she could do nothing about the smile that came to her mouth as she replied, 'You've already seen it.'

She saw his eyes flick down to her mouth, then up again to meet her eyes, but, since she had just referred to the time—was it only Thursday morning that he'd seen two of her newly decorated rooms when he'd climbed a ladder and had subsequently let her into her sitting-room?—she could not object when he apologised in advance, 'Forgive me, but the bedroom is usually the final room I visit—not the first.' And while Pernelle was feverishly trying to think up some smart and sophisticated reply to that, 'Expecting company?' he asked.

She had two choices, she realised, to tell him 'yes' or to take his hint. She looked at him, knew she liked him, and even as she had no clue to what all this might be about, other than being a peace-offering for the brute he'd been that morning, 'Come in,' she invited, and found a couple of glasses.

They shared his wine in her sitting-room, where he declared himself most impressed that she'd actually done the paper-hanging unaided. 'I wasn't very sympathetic to what you were trying to achieve, was I?' he said softly, and such was the sudden charm of the man that Pernelle, while not quite believing it, found she was making excuses for him.

'To have some peace and quiet at weekends is no more than you should expect after a hectic week.'

'You make me sound in my dotage,' he grinned, and she fell further under the spell of his charm.

She soon discovered, however, that his real reason for calling was to ask her a favour, in that he was expecting an important parcel next week. Would she take it in if it arrived?

'Yes, of course,' she told him, wondering briefly why if it was so important he didn't have it delivered to his London home, then realising that it must be something for Myrtle Cottage—and then the time simply flew.

Pernelle made several discoveries that night. She discovered that she and Hunter shared quite a few of the same likes and dislikes. She discovered that, while they disagreed on some subjects, they could disagree, amicably. And she discovered, when he stood up and said he didn't wish to outstay his welcome, that she didn't want him to go!

Naturally, she did nothing whatsoever to detain him, but, her eye catching sight of the time by the kitchen clock as she went through with him to politely see him to the door, she was incredulous at where the last hour and a half had gone!

'You've redecorated the kitchen too, haven't you?' he enquired in passing, then half turned and was in time to witness the way her lips started to pull up at the corners in amusement.

'You—er—heard me doing it, I believe, and—er—rang me one Sunday morning to—er—mention it,' she laughed.

His eyes were still on her mouth, but then suddenly he moved his glance to her large brown eyes. 'Did I once call you incorrigible?' he queried.

'I believe you may have done,' she replied mock-demurely, and felt her heart give an energetic flutter of delight when he laughed.

Her smile departed as swiftly as his, though, when, his expression all at once serious, he took hold of her by her upper arms. Then, as her breath caught, his head came down.

But as if he sensed a certain tension, a stiffness in her, and maybe thought she was still not quite over her experience with her date of last evening—Pernelle was suddenly too shaken to be able to tell what exactly—he unexpectedly pulled back at the last moment and eased his hold on her upper arms.

Then, again looking into her eyes, he murmured quietly, 'Goodnight, Pernelle Richards.'

'Goodnight,' she answered huskily, and stood still and unmoving when lightly, gently, he touched his lips to hers.

She stood exactly where he had left her for quite some minutes after she'd heard him let himself into his own home. Then, slowly, she went upstairs and got ready for bed.

Half an hour later she was in bed, and her most shattering discovery of all that evening was still there, and was no figment of her imagination. That most shattering discovery—that she was in love with Hunter Tremaine!

CHAPTER SIX

PERNELLE awoke on Monday morning and had no need to wonder any longer why Hunter was so much on her mind. She now knew exactly what was the matter with her and exactly why she couldn't get him off her mind. She was in love with him, and could no longer hide from that fact.

She lay for a while straining her ears for any sign of a sound from next door, but she could hear not a sound, and, feeling suddenly deflated, she left her bed to get on with her day.

She drank a cup of tea, knowing by then that Hunter must have already departed for London. She took her shower and felt decidedly Monday-morningish at the thought that it would be a whole five days, *at least*, before she saw him again.

Perhaps she wasn't feeling so energetic that morning, but she was a few minutes later than usual when she locked her back door after her and went out to her car—then stopped dead. Hunter's garage doors were open! Her heart suddenly started to race, when first she heard the purr of the Jaguar's engine, then saw it being reversed out of the garage.

Shyness, that same idiotic shyness which she would swear she had never been prone to before, made her turn her back on the Jaguar and its driver, and attend to unlocking her car for all the world as though she hadn't heard it. She took a few deep breaths. Then, since it was obvious that she could not avoid hearing him leave his car and close his garage doors, hoping to appear natural, she turned around.

She saw Hunter, dear, marvellous, wonderful Hunter, striding to his car. Clearly he was in a hurry. But not, she discovered happily, in too much of a hurry to flick a glance her way.

'Your car all right now?' he pleasantly passed the time of day.

'I had it fixed, thanks,' she smiled, and, as he got into his car, so she got into hers. He had driven down to his gates, opened them and closed them after him and was away by the time she got down to hers. Pernelle sighed, but felt less out of sorts than she had, as she drove to work.

'Did Mr Tremaine come down this weekend?' was one of the first questions Mike asked when she got in.

Did he ever? 'He—er—came down on Saturday—er—morning,' Pernelle replied, and realised that there must have been something defensive in her attitude when Mike looked at her quite edgily.

'But you didn't exchange cross words?' he questioned anxiously.

She didn't need to think back to recall the way Hunter had seen Chris Farmer off her premises on Saturday night, or the way he had so comfortingly cradled her afterwards.

'Oh, no,' she answered Mike blithely, and when, satisfied, he went off to his own office, she fell into happy thoughts of the weekend. She relived every moment of the harmonious hour and a half she had spent with Hunter last night, which had ended with him lightly kissing her and with her facing what had been waiting to be acknowledged for some time now—that she was in love with him. The fact that on Saturday they had reared up at each other when sheep had got into his garden via hers, and that on Sunday they'd clashed again when he'd objected to her erecting an eyesore of a fence, passed her by.

Hunter was much on her mind that day. Tuesday was just the same, with the morning starting off with Mike trying to hold down his excitement at a letter he had received from Braddon Consolidated, and which Hunter had personally signed.

'I know Braddons aren't offering the backing but merely setting out their criteria for doing so,' Mike dissected the letter. 'But they're not slamming the door on me like everybody else, are they?' he exclaimed excitedly. 'They're leaving it wide open!'

'Er—it seems that way!' Pernelle offered hesitantly.

'Don't you see,' Mike was too excited to allow hesitancy, 'that men like Hunter Tremaine don't put their signatures on letters like this one unless they're very seriously considering the venture?'

'You're right, of course,' she had to agree, and while Mike went off to phone his wife, more cheered than he'd been in a long while, Pernelle, foolishly searching for every crumb, she freely owned, fell to wondering if Hunter had given one thought to her, no matter how tiny that thought was, when writing to her boss.

She went home that night knowing that she was being utterly ridiculous. It was completely absurd, for goodness' sake, that a man as busy as he must be should have time to pause and remember that he was acquainted with the secretary of the man he was writing to.

Then joy, utter joy, filled her as, having firmly rejected any notion that Hunter had given her a thought during his working day, she had evidence, when her phone rang, that he had a moment to think of her in the evening.

For it was about seven that evening that she answered her phone, and, albeit it was more the parcel he was expecting that Hunter was interested in, her heart leapt just to hear him.

'Hello, Pernelle,' he greeted her. 'Hunter Tremaine,' he announced himself, needlessly, since her skin had begun to tingle from just that *'hello'*. 'How's the weather your way of the world?' he asked conversationally, and her heart lifted as she realised he didn't seem in any hurry to get his call over.

'What do you expect in the middle of summer?' she replied lightly.

'Raining there too, huh?'

'Real welly weather,' she answered, and, wanting to keep him talking as long as possible but not wanting him to know that, 'Your parcel hasn't arrived,' she volunteered. 'I've looked all round, but there's no sign of it.'

'Did you look in my shed? I left it unlocked purposely,' he informed her.

'Yes, I did,' she told him, then thought she hadn't sounded very friendly and almost went to try to redress the balance by telling him she had typed a letter to him that day stating Mike's acceptance of Braddons' criteria and conditions should they wish to put some finance into his business. Somehow, though, she discovered that she didn't want anything to do with work to interfere with what was a—private chat. 'Perhaps it will come tomorrow,' she suggested, letting a smile come into her voice.

'I hope so,' Hunter replied warmly, and rang off. Pernelle put down her receiver and for the next thirty minutes sat smiling into space.

She had pulled herself back together again by morning, and could only wonder at the idiot love had made of her. But even while she owned that it was little short of ridiculous to sit smiling into space for half an hour after a simple enquiry about a parcel, that did not stop her thinking constantly about Hunter.

Indeed, he was so much in her thoughts that she had no need to be reminded of him when, midway through some dictation that morning, Mike broke off, to comment, 'Mr Tremaine should have received my letter by now, don't you think?'

'Er—if the post's behaving itself, I should think so,' she replied, and recognised that Mike's anxiety was back. And suddenly she began to feel a most dreadful conflict of interests. She knew full well the tremendous relief it would be to her employer to have Hunter's company agree the loan, yet all at once she felt unable to so much as casually mention that Hunter had telephoned last night about a parcel he was expecting.

They resumed work, and she later went back to her desk to wonder about this protective feeling that had come over her to want to shield Hunter, who must work so hard, from any intrusion into his spare time and private life.

She drove home that evening wishing those two words 'private life' had never entered her head. For, with those two words, jealousy had entered her soul. And, even though she knew it was laughable to think he was anything else but a free agent—and what had it got to do with her anyway, for goodness' sake?—jealousy tortured her whenever she thought of his women. She knew of two, who trotted up his garden path on a Saturday, and for a while dwelt seriously on the notion of going to see her mother and stepfather this weekend.

Pernelle let herself into Primrose Cottage and faced the fact that, even if there might be a third and new female trotting up the drive of Myrtle Cottage this weekend, she would have to stay. Painful though she would find it, her love for Hunter demanded that, if he was coming down to Chumleigh Edge this weekend, she should be there too.

Having decided on that, she also decided that she, nevertheless, was not going to be anybody's doormat. There'd been no parcel post delivery first thing that morning, but she'd be blowed if she'd go looking to see if his parcel had arrived by second post.

Her resolve stayed firm all the way through the light meal she made and then ate. Though by the time she had washed up the dishes she was beginning to waver. Hunter had phoned at seven last night, she recalled without difficulty, and, although she was certain he would not ring again tonight, suddenly, at twenty to seven, she was electrified into action.

A thorough search of all nooks and crannies, however, revealed that the awaited parcel had still not arrived. At seven o'clock Pernelle was seated in her sitting-room, unable to resist a glance at the telephone every now and then. At five past seven, she knew he was not going to ring. The weather had cleared up, and at ten past seven, firmly determining that she had been ridiculous for long enough, Pernelle decided she would do some gardening. She stood up, her phone rang—and her legs turned to jelly.

She went over to the phone and picked it up and, knowing it wouldn't be Hunter, strove to keep her voice normal lest anyone who knew her well thought there was something the matter. 'Hello,' she said brightly.

'The weather's improved, I take it!' Hunter remarked.

'Sorry?' she queried, sinking down into a chair before her legs gave way.

'There's sunshine in your voice,' he teased, and she loved him.

She swallowed, then answered, 'Some days are like that.'

'You've had a good day?' he questioned, but Pernelle didn't want to talk about work.

'Not bad—I was just about to get cracking in the garden,' she replied off the top of her head.

'Nothing I said, I hope?' He stayed teasing, and Pernelle, who remembered how he'd once made her furious when he'd crustily suggested that some labour in her garden would not come amiss, actually heard herself laugh.

Oh, heavens, she thought a moment later, to her ears, even her laugh sounding loving—which was quite enough to stop her. 'Your parcel didn't arrive, by the way,' she thought she'd better tell him, then hated her impetuosity, for, the subject changed, the laughter gone, the teasing gone, Hunter thanked her nicely and rang off.

He was still in her thoughts as she drove to her office the next morning. Again no parcel had arrived for him, but she mustn't start thinking he would ring her again that evening to check. That way lay disappointment.

Hunter, she soon discovered, was on someone else's mind too, very much so. For barely had she got in and exchanged a few friendly words with Mike than he was commenting, 'I wonder if Mr Tremaine will be coming down to his home at Chumleigh Edge this weekend.'

His house next door to me, you mean, Pernelle thought, and suddenly began to feel that Mike was pressurising her. 'I—er—suppose there's a fair chance,' she replied quietly, and didn't need the extra stress of guilt that she felt unable to open up and tell him that Hunter had telephoned last night.

She left her office at five that evening and went home to check before she went in if there had been a parcel post delivery. There had not, and she let herself into her home, striving with all she had not to listen for the phone. He wouldn't ring. Or would he? This parcel seemed important.

At ten past seven, when her nerves were stretched and her palms quite moist, the phone rang. All smart re-hearsed topics of conversation abruptly disappeared from her head as she picked up the phone, and said, 'Hello,' from a dry throat.

'Hello, love,' her mother answered.

Pernelle gave herself a quick mental shake to think she should, in this instance, feel disappointed that it was her mother on the telephone. 'So what's wrong?' she pulled herself together to tease.

'Can't a mother speak with her daughter on the phone twice in one week without there being something wrong?' her mother replied with a light laugh, but went on to tell her more seriously that Mrs Deakin, her next-door neighbour, had gone into hospital to have hip replacement surgery and, since Mrs Deakin seemed short on family and friends, to ask if Pernelle would send her a get-well card to cheer her up.

'Of course I will,' Pernelle obliged, remembering Mrs Deakin from the time she'd taken her dog Arthur out for a walk. 'Have you got her hospital address?' During the next minute Pernelle wrote down the ward Mrs Deakin was in and the hospital, then asked, 'Is Arthur in kennels?'

'He was, but he broke out,' and while Pernelle just had to laugh at the picture her mother had stirred in her mind of the rough-haired Jack Russell terrier not thinking too much of his new abode, and escaping, her mother was going on, 'Mrs Deakin had him taken to the kennels the day before she was due to go into hospital, so you can imagine how upset she was when that same night she heard him barking and scratching at the door to be let in.'

'Oh, the poor dear!' Pernelle sympathised, but had started to guess the answer even as she asked, 'Where's Arthur now?'

'At this precise moment, he's taking Bruce for a walk.'

'He's staying with you?'

'Mrs Deakin was so distressed, I couldn't do anything else but offer.'

Her mother, Pernelle discovered, was in a chatty mood. Bruce was thinking seriously of selling his business and in fact had had an offer, his sister Beryl was unwell, but nothing too serious. And, saving the best until last, her mother related how once everything to do with the business was completed, she and Bruce were going to take a world cruise.

'That sounds exciting!' Pernelle said warmly.

'Oh, it won't be for ages y...' Her mother broke off. Then, 'I can hear Arthur barking!' She came back on the line saying, 'He's such a holy terror, I shall have to go and find out what he's been up to this time.'

No sooner had Pernelle put the phone down than it rang again. She had the earpiece automatically up to her ear when, before she could so much as get a word out, Hunter Tremaine rapped, 'You've been on the phone a long time!'

'I—er...' Pernelle blinked at his accusing tone, and for an idyllic moment or two was enchanted by the thought that he sounded jealous! Almost immediately she cancelled out any such ridiculous notion. He wasn't jealous, for heaven's sake! What he was, most likely, was impatient to get his call about his expected parcel over, because he'd got a date that night. That was when her own jealousy took over. 'It's all right with you if I chat to my mother from time to time, I hope?' she queried, making no apology for her sarcasm.

'So I've had a bad day,' he replied, to her surprise not slamming the phone down on her, or coming back with something doubly sarcastic, but, to cause her temper to evaporate into thin air, as good as apologising for his curt tone.

'I'm sorry to add to your bad day,' she instantly capitulated, 'but your parcel still hasn't arrived.'

'Hmm,' he grunted, but sounded quite pleasant when he remarked, 'I'll have to get my secretary to chase it up.'

There seemed little she could reply to that. Yet, when she wanted to keep him talking, the only thing that came into her head was to wonder if she should ask him if his company had come to a decision about Mike Yolland Plastics yet. Horrified that, when Hunter had just this minute told her he'd had a bad day, she should be on the brink of discussing work when he must want a break from it, she quickly changed tack. 'Perhaps your parcel will come tomorrow,' she said, then, afraid her tongue might run away with her yet, she said a friendly 'Goodnight,' and rang off.

She spent some time after Hunter's call in shakenly reflecting that it was only yesterday that she'd discovered in herself a protective feeling of wanting to zealously guard Hunter's leisure time. Yet, only a day later, she had nearly asked outright how Mike's application for some backing was going on. Pernelle went out and did some gardening, fully aware then that the pressure of Mike's anxieties over the future of his firm must be getting to her more than she'd thought.

Pernelle stirred on Friday morning and, for the first time in an age, felt she'd rather not have to go to work. She felt well, but confused, torn in two, her unquestionable loyalty to Mike suddenly in question.

She attempted to get clear of her confusion, and the feeling that she was being disloyal, by analysing that it couldn't be wrong not to tell Mike about Hunter's phone calls. They were personal—well, personal-ish. So the reason why she didn't want Mike to know about those calls, she analysed honestly, was from fear that he would think she was more friendly than she was—and might want her to take advantage of that friendship to find out how things were going.

He was as good as asking that anyway, she realised when she went into Mike's office to go through the post. 'Nothing from Braddon Consolidated yet!' he told her with a heavy sigh, having been in early to snatch up any likely-looking envelope. Then, looking directly at her, 'I expect you'll be seeing Mr Tremaine at some time over the weekend?'

'I expect so—if he comes down,' she answered quietly, and felt dreadful, guilty and mean, that she felt totally unable to offer to approach Hunter on his behalf. 'We—er—don't always hit it off, Mike, you know that,' she reminded him.

'That's true,' he remembered, and Pernelle felt worse than ever when he added, 'Perhaps it'll be as well left alone.'

'Couldn't you ring Braddons?' she suggested.

'Not without losing face,' he replied, going on, 'I don't know, Pernelle, I somehow have a gut feeling that Hunter

Tremaine wouldn't have written personally had the backing I'm after been out of the question. It's just the waiting for confirmation that's driving me up the wall!'

At one o'clock Pernelle went out to lunch and posted off a get-well card to Mrs Deakin, in a very sombre mood. She returned to her desk to spend a very unhappy time of it, being torn inside out until in the end she had convinced herself that she owed Mike more than she was giving.

She went into his office at a few minutes before five. 'If I get the chance, Mike, shall I ask Mr Tremaine how things are progressing?'

She felt she had done right when the first smile she had seen on him all day peeped out. 'I'd be glad if you would,' he replied.

If she did not look forward to carrying out the task she had volunteered to do, then Pernelle felt marginally happier on going home than she had done. Seven o'clock came and went, then half past seven, and there was no telephone call from Hunter seeking his missing parcel. She owned to feeling shaky inside—all augured well for Hunter to arrive at some time tonight.

When her phone rang at about twenty to eight, she wasn't sure which emotion was uppermost, dejection that he wouldn't be coming down, or suppressed excitement that she was going to speak to him.

Both emotions were rendered void, however, for on answering the phone, she discovered that there were other people who knew her phone number besides him.

''Lo, Pernelle,' Julian Collins' friendly tones greeted her.

'How's Julian?' she dredged up a cheerful note to ask lightly.

'Having a tantrum,' he confessed jokingly, and went on to reveal how he'd been all set to take some girl to a play at the Unicorn Theatre in East Durnley tomorrow evening, but that she'd just rung up to say she'd got 'flu.

'How inconsiderate of her!' Pernelle teased, and knew before he asked that she didn't want to go to the theatre tomorrow but wanted to stay home, in case, on the very remotest of all remote possibilities, Hunter came round with a bottle of wine and asked, 'Want to show me your decorating?'

'You wouldn't come with me, would you—if you've nothing else on, of course?' Julian asked hopefully, and Pernelle went into a rapid assessment of how love for Hunter had caused her to feel disloyal to her boss, and how the same love was now causing her to feel on the verge of being disloyal to her friends.

'So what time?' she asked.

'Oh, you are good!' Julian said in delight. 'For that I'll buy you a gin in the interval.'

'You certainly know how to treat a girl,' she joked, and rang off, having arranged for him to pick her up at seven-fifteen, and to go to her window and wonder what time Hunter would arrive.

Pernelle did not sleep well that night. Hunter had not arrived, but that did not stop her hoping. He had arrived around four o'clock one Saturday morning, she remembered.

Four o'clock came and then half past, and there was no click of his gate, or the purr of his Jaguar. She got out of bed on Saturday morning, and sat downstairs with a cup of tea, and just didn't know how she would bear it if he didn't come down at all that weekend.

After her shower Pernelle donned shorts and a cotton top, then, needing some kind of activity, she set to work vacuuming and cleaning her two-up, two-down dwelling.

At a quarter to eleven, and in a conscious endeavour to cure her habit, born that morning, of looking out through front room windows to see what cars were about—in particular, Jaguars—she went and got the lawnmower out. Then, when her grass needed cutting, as if to prove just how unsettled she was feeling, she went indoors, deciding she would have a coffee break first.

Hunter should be here by now if he was coming, she fretted dispiritedly, and while she experienced such a desperate longing to see him, she suddenly started to have the most dreadful feeling that she wouldn't see him at all that weekend.

The thought that he was staying in London and would not be coming down to Chumleigh Edge all at once seemed a definite possibility. And if that wasn't enough to contend with, Pernelle was suddenly eaten up by jealousy that, of course, some female—sophisticated and elegant, naturally—was the cause.

The kettle boiled, she went over to it, and was deep in unhappy thought that Hunter had probably had such a heavy date last night that he... when just as she raised the kettle and started to pour boiling water over the granules in the cup, her other hand absently adding a spoon to the saucer, Hunter walked by her open kitchen window.

At that same moment a small cry of alarm escaped her. For, even while her heart began to swell with happiness, she made an involuntary movement of total surprise and succeeded in pouring boiling water, not over the coffee granules, but over her hand.

So quickly then that she barely knew what was happening, Hunter was inside her kitchen and while, still shaken, she stared from her injured hand to him and back to her left hand again, he had taken everything in, and was at once in charge.

And before she knew it, while filling her washing up bowl with cold water, he was holding her hand under the cold tap, and then, the bowl full, he pushed her hand down into the bowl.

Feeling stunned, bemused, Pernelle looked up at him and searched for some sort of normality. But how could she possibly find normality in this abnormal situation—particularly when Hunter was standing with his left arm kindly about her shoulders?

As she stared mutely up at him, though, so Hunter stared down at her. Then, the corners of his mouth starting to turn up, 'Good morning, Miss Richards,' he greeted her.

'G... I d-didn't hear you arrive!' she stammered, and wanted the ground to open up and swallow her if he should get the idea that she'd been listening for him. 'The wall—in between—it's so thin...' she began to explain, but broke off, tensing up when suddenly her injured hand started to burn like crazy.

She closed her eyes to try to hide from him the pain she was in, and then realised that he knew anyway, for, gently, his other arm came about her and he encircled her in a comforting hold.

'Think of England,' he teased softly, compassionately, and held her close.

Magically then, as he dropped a light kiss on top of her head, some of the pain disappeared. When a few seconds later he feathered a light kiss on the side of her face, pain seemed incidental.

She pulled her head back and found she was looking up into his eyes. 'You're quite beautiful,' he murmured, and her heart raced, as he kissed her. It was a deeply satisfying kiss, full of warmth and tenderness, and Pernelle was very nearly devastated by it by the time Hunter pulled back.

'Er—*quite* beautiful?' she questioned, as she fought desperately hard to pull herself together again.

'Quite superbly featured and shaped. Beautiful is no exaggeration,' he breathed, and kissed her again.

Wrapped in his arms where she wanted to be, his lips on hers what she wanted, Pernelle saw no reason to hold back, and responded wholeheartedly. Never had she felt like this about anyone.

When he eventually broke that kiss, he looked down into her flushed face and melting eyes for a few long and tense moments. Then, 'Your hand's supposed to be in the water, not around my neck,' he murmured lightly.

Pernelle had no memory whatsoever of taking her hand out of the bowl of water. 'Your shirt's—er—wet,' she mumbled, and when he grinned endearingly, so endearingly, down at her, she took a step back and then another, out of his arms, and fought the hardest she had ever fought to counteract the nonsense he had just made her. By some good fortune, she found that her voice had just the right amount of dryness to it as she told him, 'You're certainly up to date with your cures!'

'I'm thinking of putting up a brass plate,' he returned, and she loved him, and could do nothing but burst out laughing.

When he laughed too, and took a step towards her, her heart started to race again. She knew he was going to take her in his arms again—and that she could not, and did not, want to do anything to stop him.

It was Hunter himself, however, who called a halt. For suddenly he was shaking his head, and then, with a rueful look at her, 'Better not,' he commented, and, taking a few steps away, abruptly steered into less hazardous waters by completely changing direction to enquire, 'Any parcel for me?'

'Sorry,' she replied, and desperately tried to pull herself together. She turned, and, her glance lighting on the kettle, the cause of all the trouble, 'I was in the act of making a cup of coffee,' she told him from a sudden necessity to say something. And, though what she needed above all else was to be by herself, she asked, 'Would you like one?'

'I'll make it,' he volunteered. 'You sit down and rest that hand,' and somehow, though she'd had no intention of complying, she found she was doing exactly that.

While he was busy making the coffee, though, Pernelle was beset by real fears that he might have guessed, from her response to him just now, that there was more there than just the circumstance of the moment.

She was, therefore, in an agitated state. What the deuce, she wondered, could she say to him that might cancel out any notion he had that she might care very deeply for him? At that moment he came over and placed a cup of coffee on the kitchen table beside her. Unthinkingly, she had both her hands idly on the table when he took the chair at the other side of the table. She saw he was studying the redness of her left hand, but, not wanting to make a big issue of it by trying to hide her hand, she left it where it was.

Most casually then, he looked from her hand to her face. 'You should be all right for your date tonight,' he commented.

Thank you, Hunter, Pernelle thought, having just been presented with one very quick way of showing him that, when it came to caring deeply, there were other men in her life.

'I'll be fine,' she replied brightly. 'Not that I'm doing anything more strenuous than going to the theatre.'

'Not with the same man you dated last Saturday, I hope!' Hunter barked harshly—unfortunately, his tone at once causing her to react sharply.

'Do credit me with *some* sense!' she bit, and when he scowled heavily, she waited for the explosion.

It did not come, but, his glance flicking from her angry expression to the angry look of her left hand, he seemed to swallow what he'd been about to lambast her with, and, downing his coffee in one go, he stood up to instruct, 'Take some aspirin—you'll feel better!' Then, as cool as you like, he strolled out.

Was there ever a man to make you feel like loving him and hating him all at the one time? Pernelle wondered, having not taken kindly to his, 'Take some aspirin—you'll feel better!' Just as though everything was her fault! Not that there was anything to be anybody's fault about, she fumed and, ignoring the aspirin bottle, went out to mow her back lawn.

By the time Julian came to call for her that night Pernelle had forgotten all her scratchy thoughts and feelings about Hunter, and was head over heels in love with him again. Dressed in a silky two-piece of royal blue, she had taken some care with her appearance, but there was no sign of Hunter anywhere when she and Julian went down the drive.

The play, as plays went, was average. 'Now for that gin I promised,' Julian laughed when the interval came. And, 'Thank the lord I still play rugger!' he exclaimed when they reached the refreshment area and, hunching his shoulders, he went off to the bar, while Pernelle went deep into Hunter Tremaine territory.

Hoping with all her might that by telling him about her date she had hit on the head any idea he might have gleaned that she was a one-man woman and that that one man was him, she was suddenly shaken to the core when a splendid voice asked, 'All alone?'

Turning rapidly round, she could hardly believe her eyes. What was Hunter doing here? On the heels of that, though—and she appreciated that Hunter could mix up her thinking like no one else—she had the craziest notion that he'd followed her just to check that she did indeed have a date. 'You never said anything about coming here tonight!' she erupted—and was at once horrified by her challenging tone, and mortified to realise belatedly how ridiculous was any such notion that he would be anywhere because of her!

But by then, his right eyebrow going aloft at her impudence, Hunter was taking the sarcastic route to flatten her challenge. 'Surprising as it may seem,' he rapped, 'I don't have to tell you everything!'

She'd asked for that, she knew she had, but that, to her way of thinking, was no reason why she should crumple into a humiliated heap. 'Oh, you're impossible!' she snapped—and was never more glad when, just then, Julian returned.

Though had she thought that Julian's being there might prevent Hunter from having the last word, she was very much mistaken. For, 'Impossible, am I?' he questioned, and added, deliberately, she knew, 'I'll remember that the next time you plead with me to enter your bedroom!' And, having delivered that little gem, and while Pernelle went scarlet—certain that everyone else had heard—he waited for her reply, and when none came—she was truly silenced—he nodded, ignored her escort, and walked away.

When, Pernelle wondered furiously, had she ever thought of him as anything other than a vile swine?

CHAPTER SEVEN

PERNELLE was still furious with Hunter when she awoke the next morning. He *was* a swine, there was no getting away from it. There had been no need for him to say what he had last night, no need at all.

She got out of bed and went downstairs to make some tea, still railing against him, and wishing he'd taken himself off to some other theatre last night. East Durnley only had one theatre, though—which in no way explained why, having told him that she was going to the theatre, she had jumped to the ludicrous conclusion that he was only there because he knew she'd be at the Unicorn Theatre last night.

Ludicrous didn't begin to cover her wild, albeit only momentary assumption that he was there checking that she really did have a date. Pernelle clattered about with china as though hoping to drown out her thoughts. But she had soon come full circle, and was again furious with Hunter and his flattening, 'I'll remember that the next time you plead with me to enter your bedroom' remark. Thank goodness Julian was Julian, and once she'd explained how it had all come about that she'd 'pleaded' with her neighbour to 'enter her bedroom', he, like the good friend he was, believed her unquestioningly. Tremaine wasn't to know that, though, was he?

The more Pernelle thought about it, the more she saw that, had she had any serious relationship going with her date of last night, in that one squashing sentence Hunter Tremaine could have ruined it.

Once showered, she got dressed and, noticing that it looked like being a beautiful sunny day, went around opening windows, then did a few chores. Then she recalled how yesterday she had tackled her rear lawn and garden, with the idea of having a go at the front lawn today. But—she hesitated.

Minutes later, however, mutiny had entered her soul. Damn him, she'd done nothing wrong! She wouldn't hide away, she just wouldn't.

Not much longer afterwards, Pernelle was clattering her not-so-new lawnmower round to the front of her cottage. A surreptitious glance at her neighbour's property showed that he had most of his windows open too. Good. Although it was now past ten, she hoped he was having a lie-in.

There was something very satisfying to be found in the noise an old lawnmower made as it rattled over an old lawn, she decided. Having trundled it up towards her cottage, she turned and was about to mow down another strip when the machine suddenly became grass-clogged.

To unclog it did not take long, but, as she straightened up, a phone rang. For a moment she thought it was the phone in her sitting-room, but as she took a step to answer it, the ringing stopped and she clearly heard Hunter in his sitting-room announce, 'Tremaine.'

She glanced at his sitting-room window, but could not see him, and quickly looked away again. She turned her back on the two cottages and took hold of the lawn-mower again. But, just as she was about to begin pushing it down to the bottom hedge, she became riveted by what Hunter was saying.

'Lily!' he exclaimed in pleasure when his caller must have announced herself. 'How very nice of you to ring,' he added. There was a small silence then, while Lily obviously gave him some reason for calling, then while Pernelle started to feel quite ill, and clutched hard on to the handle of the lawnmower, 'Do you really want me to come?' she heard him ask, such a teasing note in his voice that Pernelle realised he just had to know Lily extremely well! Then, when she must clearly have been pleading with him to come and see her, he gave in, with the warmth of a smile in his voice. 'For you, sweetheart, anything,' he said, and, while Pernelle felt just as if a knife had turned in her, 'I'll be there around twelve-thirty,' he added, and ended the call.

Pernelle at once got busy pushing her mower down to the bottom hedge. He was good at getting women to plead with him, was Tremaine, she thought, trying quite desperately to get angry. She needed to be angry—anything was better than this dreadful pain inside.

But she couldn't feel angry, and she turned at the bottom of her front lawn and mowed her way to the top, then turned about again, feeling her heart was about to break.

When at the bottom of her lawn she did another about-turn, though, and started once more on her way up, she saw that, as if from nowhere, a couple of canvas chairs had appeared on the gravel at the top.

Her heart was soon thundering away, though she knew that thundering had nothing to do with her labour of pushing such an old machine. She tried to appear cool, however, so it was without stopping that on gaining the top of the lawn she did another about-turn.

She did several more turns, one more at the top, and two at the bottom. And it was at that last about-turn,

as she was again making her way up to the top, that
Hunter suddenly appeared bearing a tray of coffee.

Swiftly she lowered her eyes and had about a minute
in which to decide how she was going to act. To go for
his jugular at the thought that there was no end to the
females in his harem would be much too revealing, she
realised. As she realised also that revealing too would
be anything but a kind of civilised neighbourliness. The
last thing this totally unconcerned Don Juan was going
to know was that here was another victim who was
bleeding inside about him.

At the top of her lawn she looked over, to where he
was now seated on one of the opened-out canvas chairs—
on her land—and was looking over her way. She halted,
and opened her mouth to make some sort of comment,
but was saved the necessity when he remarked, 'I owe
you one.'

Realising that he must be meaning he owed her a coffee
in return for the one he'd had—and made—in her kitchen
yesterday, Pernelle went over to the other canvas chair.

'I reckon I've earned five minutes,' she commented
affably, and took her ease in the chair while Hunter
passed a cup of coffee over to her.

'How's your hand?' he enquired, and took a glance
down at it as though to ascertain for himself.

'I'll be able to type tomorrow,' she answered lightly,
and took a sip of her coffee, but, with work vaguely
there somewhere in her head, belatedly remembered that
she had promised Mike she would ask Hunter how things
were progressing—if she got the chance. 'Talking of . . .'
she began, since here was that chance—only Hunter
asked something at the same moment.

'What did you think of the play?' he wanted to know,
and she was so taken aback that he could actually *refer*

to last night—without so much as batting an eyelid either—that Mike and the question she wanted to ask Hunter went straight out of her head.

The nerve of the man! The unmitigated nerve! But she wouldn't be drawn—that way would lead her into losing her temper territory, when lord knew what snippet she'd reveal to feel mortified about forever afterwards. So she shrugged. 'I've seen better,' she replied pleasantly, and sipped some more of her coffee.

There was a pause while she surveyed her garden, then, his nerve more than unmitigated, 'Usually with the same man you were with last night?' he asked, and again Pernelle had to struggle to find some control.

In the end she was glad she managed it, because it suddenly dawned on her that Hunter was not so much interested in talking about the play, her escort, or anything at all to do with last night but that, having decided he owed her a cup of coffee, he was filling the time in while she drank it, with a few throwaway questions.

'Julian and I often go to the theatre together,' she replied and, just in case Hunter thought he'd ruined her relationship with Julian with his 'plead with me to enter your bedroom' comment—not that he'd give a damn if he had— 'We're going to see the new production at the Unicorn next Saturday, actually,' she lied smilingly, but saw that Hunter was barely interested in what lies she told. He had nothing to say in answer, anyhow, but flicked a frowning glance away from her and seemed to find her old lawnmower worthy of some study. Pernelle needed no bigger hint than that. 'Thanks for the coffee,' she said in chirrupy fashion, and, placing her coffee-cup and saucer on the tray, she got up and ambled back to her labours.

She later watched Hunter drive off to his assignation with Lily, and, while loving him, hated him that he could go to some other woman. Pernelle did not feel in the least like gardening after that—or like doing anything else either, for that matter. But doggedly she set about the weeds which seemed to have sprung up overnight, and tried to get him out of her mind.

In trying to pin her thoughts elsewhere, she thought of Mike, and while she thought that it was doubtful that Hunter would return that weekend, it started to prey on her mind that the first thing Mike was going to ask tomorrow was—what did Mr Tremaine say?

An hour later she was still feeling bad about Mike, and positive that Hunter's date was with some woman who lived in London—which would cause him to see no point in returning to Chumleigh Edge before next weekend.

At four o'clock she gave up gardening, washed her hands and went up to the village shop in the hope that they'd still got a Sunday paper. Since she'd had it with gardening and anything else today, she decided she'd have a bath, read the paper, do the crossword and, if at all possible, try to think up what to tell Mike tomorrow that would excuse the way he would think she had let him down.

With her heart not really in anything, the following five or six hours dragged at a snail's pace for Pernelle. She sat for as long as she could over a light tea, then read almost every word of the newspaper she bought. She later soaked in her bath for longer than was normal, then decided to wash her hair. With the aid of a dryer it was soon dry, and, having donned a freshly laundered nightshirt, Pernelle shrugged into a light cotton robe and went downstairs.

At half past nine she drew the curtains in the sitting-room and settled down cosily on her inherited large and roomy settee with the paper folded at the crossword page.

Twenty minutes later she was still trying with all her might to keep her thoughts from straying all the while to Hunter when suddenly, in the stillness of the night, she heard the purr of a car engine. The vehicle slowed, then stopped. Hardly daring to believe what she wanted to believe, she concentrated solely on the sounds outside her cottage. Then joy, unbelievable joy flooded her heart as she heard the click of a gate. Hunter was home!

For quite some minutes, as she listened to sounds of Hunter opening his garage doors and putting his car away, she rejoiced in the fact that he had returned. He hadn't stayed in London, he hadn't stayed with Lily, he had come back to Chumleigh Edge—and to her.

It was the last thought that brought Pernelle back to reality with a start. For heaven's sake, had she gone soft in the head? Hunter hadn't come back to *her*!

During the next five minutes, as she heard Hunter let himself into Myrtle Cottage and heard him moving around in his sitting-room, Pernelle gave herself the sternest of lectures. Hunter had not come home *to her*, nor was he ever likely to *come home to her*! And, what was more, he had probably had such a whale of a time that day that he had forgotten *her* existence.

A moment later she was wondering why she should think he would remember her existence anyway—when all at once she heard the sound of his front door being closed! A moment after that, and she heard the sound of his tread on the gravel that fronted the two cottages—it was coming *nearer*!

Pernelle, as though suddenly electrified, rocketed to her feet and was standing stunned when the sound of his footsteps passed in front of her window, then halted. When his short rap on her door immediately followed, she felt rooted to the spot.

Only the fear that he might go away again if she didn't soon go and answer his knock gave her release to go swiftly to the door. To know that he was at the other side and that any moment, after these long hours of nothingness, she would see him, caused her to swallow. Then her hand went to the door catch, and she pulled it back.

He was tall, immaculately suited, and she loved him. As she rested her eyes on him, though, he rested his eyes on her, and suddenly Pernelle was overwhelmingly aware of her shiny make-up-free face and night attire, and she felt thoroughly tongue-tied.

But not so her ten o'clock caller. 'Did I say you were beautiful?' he enquired, his voice soft, and it seemed to her that the words were leaving him involuntarily. 'Correction, Pernelle,' he added, 'you're sensational!'

Her legs suddenly felt boneless and unable to support her. Oh, don't, oh, don't, she wanted to tell him, don't say such lovely things to me. But, when she suddenly found she had vocal release, she said nothing of the sort, but, ignoring the fact that his comments had made her legs feel weak, she questioned coolly, 'Have you been at the grape?'

'Two glasses of champagne with my lunch, but that was hours and hours ago,' he replied, his mouth starting to curve upwards. But Pernelle turned swiftly round, not caring to hear about the liquid, the celebratory liquid by the sound of it, that he and Lily had shared at lunchtime.

'If you've come to borrow a cup of sugar, you'd better come in,' she told him over her shoulder, and had a second or two to compose herself when, closing the door behind him, he followed her further into her sitting-room.

His expression was still good-humoured, though, when she turned and, recovering from the painful nip of jealousy, looked at him enquiringly. 'I noticed your light was on,' he commented, referring to the glow from the table lamp. 'I wondered if there were any messages.'

'Messages!' she repeated, startled—suddenly she was his message taker as well as his parcel taker?

'I was half expecting a friend to drop by. I thought— if you've been gardening all day, you might have...'

'Actually——' Pernelle stopped him right there. The nerve, the... Words failed her. 'Actually,' she found a smile to repeat, 'I've been out myself.' As far as she was concerned, the village shop was 'out'.

Hunter rested a hand idly against her fireplace. 'Lunch date?' he enquired.

She opened her mouth and was ready to lie her head off rather than let him think he was the only one who had any fun. Then she discovered that while yesterday she could lie about having a date next Saturday, now, suddenly, she didn't want to lie to him—worse, she couldn't lie to him.

Which left her with nothing but pride when, even her phony smile gone, she told him haughtily, 'It's got nothing to do with you!' and saw at once that he liked neither her tone nor her manner, nor what she said.

Though it was unhurriedly that his hand left the fire-place and he straightened to stand over her and clip in short tones, 'It has everything to do with me if I'm the one who has to come and rescue you from something you can't handle!'

'*You*, rescue me!' she exclaimed. He'd been nowhere about for most of the day!

'You're suggesting you didn't need my help the other Saturday?' he gritted.

She might have done then, but not ever again. 'I don't need a—a—protector!' she snapped.

'You're sure as hell not capable of judging for yourself who you should invite in for coffee and who you shouldn't!'

'I'll learn!'

'Huh!' he grunted. 'So next time you're in at the deep end and call for help, I'm to leave you to get on with it, am I?' he snarled.

'I won't call out!' she retorted, and, with more temper than prudence, 'I'm twenty-two now, it's time I knew more of the world,' she added uppishly, but, at the sudden demoniacal look that came into Hunter's eyes as, chin jutting, he moved a few paces nearer, she began to wish she had not added anything.

Particularly did she wish that when, his eyes not leaving hers, Hunter removed his jacket, then took off his tie. In fact, she was staring at him as though hypnotised when, all at once, he reached for her and, fury clearly filling him, pulled her into his arms. 'There's no time like the present—you can start now!' he grated. In the next instant his head was coming down and his mouth was over hers.

But it wasn't a kiss like his other kisses had been. It wasn't a kind or gentle kiss, or a warm or healing kiss, but angry and brutal, and, love him though she did, Pernelle didn't want him to kiss her—not that way.

So she fought him. 'No!' she cried the moment she could, but had no time to say more, because Hunter had again claimed her lips. Nevertheless she still struggled to be free, pushing at him, pulling at him, twisting this way and that. But all that succeeded in doing was rock their balance, so that, angry though he still undoubtedly was, Hunter chose to move them both out of harm's way, and steered her to her settee.

But she had no intention at all of sitting on that settee with him. Nor did she—because she didn't get the chance! For, how she didn't know, one moment they were both vertical—and the next, she wasn't sitting but was *horizontal*—as too was Hunter.

'Stop it at once!' she cried in panic as he lay over her and anchored her body down with his.

'Do *you* have a lot to learn!' he snarled, and entirely ignored her commands, to lower his head again and claim her lips.

'Let me up!' she yelled at the next possible moment that she could.

'What happened to "It's time I knew more of the world"?' he mimicked, but she never got the chance to answer, for once more his mouth was over hers.

His mouth, his wonderful mouth, Pernelle suddenly found herself thinking, and, while she was still as hell-bent on being free as it seemed Hunter was hell-bent on not letting her free until she'd passed a few elementary exams at least in what the 'world' had to offer, all at once she discovered that her hands weren't fists any longer. Nor, she realised, were her hands punching or pushing, but were touching and holding.

'Oh—Hunter!' she cried on a kind of wail, for in truth, she no longer knew quite where she was.

Nor, when he pulled back his head to look into her worried wide brown eyes, did she know what she wanted any more when, his voice suddenly thick in his throat, he softly soothed her, 'It's all right, Pernelle. It was never my intention to rape you.'

'I—kn-know,' she replied shakily. Whatever else she did not know, that fact just then seemed to be cemented in her brain.

'You do?' he queried, a crooked sort of a smile coming to his face—and, all at once, every scrap of aggression seemed to leave him and, gently, he kissed her—and to be kissed gently by him was what she wanted.

'Oh!' she sighed, and her arms, of their own volition, went up and around him.

'Um—I think...' Hunter began when their kiss broke, but Pernelle had spent hours in a nothingness solitude that day, and it was the comfort of his lips that she wanted. So that, when he did not kiss her, she stretched up and kissed him—and what he thought never got said.

Kiss after kiss they shared, and as a fire licked into life within her, Pernelle never wanted him to go. As Hunter pressed his body against her, she pressed to get closer to him.

She knew more rapture when he traced kisses down the side of her face and throat, then buried his face in her hair. 'Your hair smells wonderful,' he breathed, and traced tiny kisses back to the corners of her mouth again. Then, as he once more claimed her mouth, his hands began to caress her body through the thin cotton of her scant clothing. 'We don't need this, do we?' he questioned, touching long sensitive fingers to her robe.

Wordlessly, she shook her head, and within seconds her robe was gone and, only from consideration for any lingering modesty she might have in these new waters, Hunter let her keep her nightshirt.

Not that it was much protection, nor did she want it to be. For, as passion soared between them once more, and those gentle kisses changed to be giving, yet demanding, she wanted to get closer to him.

His caressing hands at her back pressed her to him, and while feverishly she clung to him, those hands came round to the front of her, and caressed her breasts.

'Oh, Hunter!' she breathed.

'You're all right?' he enquired.

'Yes, oh yes!' she whispered, and clung to him some more, holding him yet tighter when his fingers came beneath her nightshirt and he stroked her body in warm, flesh-tingling movements, until he had captive the hard-peaked globes of her naked breasts.

Take me, take me, she wanted to urge, and knew when he removed his shirt that he soon would. 'My dear,' he breathed, and Pernelle felt near to fainting from the pure rapture of it.

She felt his fingers brush her thighs as he raised the hem of her nightshirt prior to removing it. But then, suddenly, he stilled. Suddenly he let go the hem of her nightshirt and, as though all at once shaken rigid, sat up. And suddenly, or so it seemed to Pernelle with her senses heightened as they had never been, he seemed totally stunned, and rocked to his very foundations.

'Hunter?' she said his name, without any knowledge of what question she was asking. Then he had not only let go of her nightshirt but had put some space between them—and that was when Pernelle began to panic with a vengeance.

He knows, she thought. He knows. He knows I'm in love with him. Oh no, oh no! Desperately she tried to pull herself together, tried to find some sort of normality. Bells were going off in her head to tell her that Hunter didn't want that sort of commitment. That he'd drop her like a hot coal if what he was thinking—that she loved him—was really true.

She looked from him down to her legs, and was shattered at how much length of thigh she was exposing. Then she knew she wasn't thinking at all clearly, for only seconds ago she had been quite ready and willing, eager even, to be without her nightshirt altogether.

Reaching to pull the nightshirt a modest inch or two down, she went to sit up at the same time that Hunter moved. The fact, though, that their joint movements had brought them close to each other again made her panic wildly. She was agitated then, too confused to know if Hunter intended to make love to her or not. But, some instinct acted for her to tell her that Hunter must never know the depths of her love for him—so it followed that she must not allow him to make love to her.

It was that same instinct, the instinct of self-preservation, she later realised, the need to put him off the scent of her love for him, which caused her to search frantically for something that had not the smallest thing to do with love—or the situation she was in. By some wild and good fortune, she found it in her employer. And she was never more grateful then that Mike and his problems must have been getting to her more than she knew, for her voice was so cool she couldn't believe it, considering the lather she was in inside; and she heard herself ask, 'Oh, by the way, have you made your decision about lending Mike the money he approached you for?'

That Hunter should look utterly astounded by her question did not surprise her. If the truth were known she was so astounded herself that she could barely believe she had just asked what she had.

She knew instantly, however, from the sudden and rampant fury on his face, that she had said entirely the wrong thing. For Hunter was on his feet, his hands snaking out to jerk her unceremoniously to her feet too. But, as a pulse throbbed violently in his temple, it suddenly seemed that he was too enraged to dare to touch her, for all at once he threw her from him and grated, 'Tell your boss, next time you see him, that Braddon Consolidated *never have*, nor *ever will*, service clients via the bedroom!'

If he'd just punched her in the stomach, Pernelle felt she could not have felt more winded. But her reaction was spontaneous none the less and not regretted when, a moment later, fury filled her at the thought that he could speak so to her, and in utter fury she lashed out and hit him full on the side of the face.

She saw his hand move from his side, and for one dreadful second she thought he was going to hit her back. But at the last moment he seemed to find a stray element of control, and his hand fell to his side.

But there was no mistaking it had been a near thing. 'That,' he clipped tautly, 'is about it!' and, gathering up his clothes in one swoop, he released the mighty passion of his violent feelings by crashing her front door unceremoniously to after him on his way out.

CHAPTER EIGHT

AFTER enduring the most tortuous night of her life, Pernelle made her way to her office on Monday having been through a whole gamut of emotions, and still feeling emotionally all over the place. Hunter was still in her head as she drove into East Durnley.

He hadn't stayed home long after he'd so furiously slammed out of her place, she recalled. Less than half an hour later she'd heard his front door bang again and, with a frantically beating heart, had thought for a few seconds that he was coming back. The next sound she'd heard, though, had been the sound of his garage doors being opened.

Her spirits had hit rock bottom when she had heard his car being driven away. All too obviously he had only returned to Myrtle Cottage for something he needed in London. Probably something he'd forgotten in his haste to join *Lily* for *lunch*, Pernelle thought sourly—then roused herself to be furious with him once more.

She was glad she had hit him! In her view he'd got off lightly. It was blatantly clear to her then that Hunter had always been going back to Lily last night. He'd only stopped by Primrose Cottage anyway to enquire if she, plainly considered a non-paid member of his staff, had any messages to pass on.

Damn him, she fumed as she pulled up and parked at Mike Yolland Plastics—and hated herself to think that while Hunter had come straight from the arms of some other woman, she had welcomed him to hers!

Pernelle got out of her car, and hated him, too, for going back to *that* other women's arms. She entered the building, feeling bruised and shaken, hurt and hating to think that Hunter, to whom she would have given herself unquestioningly, lovingly and freely, had dared to accuse her of using her body to get the loan Mike wanted. How *dared* he? He wanted stringing up!

A couple of seconds later she went into her office, and promptly had to forget her hatred—and the deep love that overrode all hatred despite anything that had happened—and all her other churned-up emotions over Hunter, for on hearing her come in, Mike came swiftly out of his office.

'Morning, Pernelle,' he greeted her, and at his tense, expectant look she realised too late that she had no excuse to offer him for the way she had let him down.

'Morning, Mike,' she answered quietly, and saw his look of hope begin to fade.

'Mr Tremaine not down this weekend?' he came straight to the point to question.

'He was,' she had to confess, and excused herself, 'But he was out for most of yesterday.'

'So you never got a chance to ask him how things were going,' he finished for her, and, making her feel dreadful when he put a brave face on it, 'Never mind, perhaps it wasn't the done thing for you to ask anyway.'

'I'm sorry, Mike,' she mumbled, feeling worse than ever.

'Forget it,' he smiled. 'I'm feeling confident anyway that Mr Tremaine wouldn't have written—or called here personally—if we didn't stand a ninety-nine-per-cent chance of doing business.'

Pernelle went back to Primrose Cottage that night with her emotions in much the same jangle that they'd been in all day. She looked round and about to see if any parcel had been delivered for Hunter, but there was no sign of a parcel. And, when she and Hunter had parted on the worst possible terms, she sat tense and with her insides knotted up when seven o'clock came—and went.

But Hunter did not telephone her that night, and she went to bed knowing she had not truly expected him to. She then spent for the most part a wakeful night with her thoughts, when not on him, on Mike, and Mike's confidence that this week, maybe next at the latest, he would be receiving a letter from Hunter offering him the finance he was after.

Thoughts of his confidence vexed her interminably. But it was in the early hours of Tuesday morning that she began to dig deeper and deeper into what she knew and what she instinctively felt to be true about Hunter. As dispassionately as possible she tried to sum up; apart from the fact that she simply couldn't believe that Hunter would be anything but fair in his dealings, she just knew he would never have got to be head of Braddons were he anything but honest and straight.

Suddenly, then, she began to feel as confident as Mike. She recalled the letter he had received from Hunter setting out Braddon Consolidated's terms for any loan, and all at once she just *knew* that Hunter wouldn't write so—not unless he intended to help Mike. At last she settled down for a little sleep.

Pernelle went to work the next morning feeling a shade more refreshed than she had the previous morning and as confident about the loan as she had been in the early hours. She went into her office, saw Mike's door was open, and called, 'Good morning, Mike!'—then had that confidence totally shattered when, grey-faced, Mike came out of his office. 'What . . .?' she asked.

Without a word he came over to her and gave her a letter he was holding in his hand. Then, while she stared at the man who seemed to look ten years older than he had yesterday, he turned and went back into his own office.

The letter, she saw, was from Braddon Consolidated. With her heart suddenly pounding, she read it, then sank disbelievingly on to a chair, to read it again. Hunter— the letter was signed personally by him—had turned Mike's application down!

How long she sat there feeling stunned, hurt, and very much let down at Hunter's 'After due consideration——' she didn't know. But again and again she read it. It still read the same—her faith in Hunter, Mike's faith in him, was all for nothing.

For an age Pernelle was stunned, but slowly she began to come out of a kind of numbness that had taken her over to wonder—as it was inevitable that she would, she later realised—if Hunter's decision had anything to do with her.

Again and again his 'Braddon Consolidated *never have*, nor *ever will*, service clients via the bedroom!' haunted her. Oh, no, he couldn't, she thought in anguish. He wouldn't penalise Mike because of her! He couldn't be so unfair—could he?

She didn't want to believe it, couldn't believe it—then she remembered the furious way she had lashed out at Hunter on Sunday. Then she looked at the date of the letter. It was dated yesterday! No, no, no, she thought brokenly, and all hell was suddenly let loose in her, as Hunter's taut parting remark of 'That is about it!' sped back to her.

His remark hadn't meant much more to her then, except that with both of them spitting fire she had used an unfair advantage in hitting him where, although she thought he'd come close to it, he couldn't hit back.

But he had hit back, hadn't he—and in a dreadfully painful way. He knew it would mean a lot to her that Mike should get this backing. But, having dangled the chance of that finance as a near certainty, what had he done? He, because of her, she was now sure, had snatched that chance back again!

Feeling utterly devastated, Pernelle felt she should go in and say something to Mike. But what could she say? Nothing she said was going to make him feel any better. And she discovered to her disgust that while something in her wanted to go honestly and confess to Mike that it was because of her he had not got the loan, she could not. For she suddenly found that, hate Hunter as she would, her loyalty to him was greater than her loyalty to her employer. So, that being the case, how could she go to Mike and let him know that Hunter was less than he thought him, by confessing that the only reason he'd turned his application down was to show her where she got off?

But the fact that she could not go to Mike and confess, though, made her furious throughout the rest of that morning. Because that, quite simply, meant that Hunter could do whatever he liked, and that she—in love with the rat—would love him still.

Love him she might, she fumed when she went out in her lunch hour, but she would never forgive him. Her fury with Hunter had not abated when she returned from lunch. When the phone on her desk rang, however, she swallowed her wrath and politely answered it—but only to be immediately incensed, for the caller was none other than Hunter himself!

Why he was bothering to ring Mike with a phony apology for 'feeling unable to recommend the loan' was beyond her, but, while her heart beat thunderously away, Pernelle strove with all her might to stay businesslike. Though she could do nothing about the frost that fairly crackled in her voice when, without pausing to enquire what he wanted, 'Mr Yolland is not available at the moment,' she told him with icy crispness. 'If you'd like to leave a...'

'I didn't call to speak to him!' Hunter cut her off, her icy crispness nothing compared to his.

The gall! The utter gall of the man! 'Then I can only assume that you've rung to speak with me!' she erupted, and as ice underwent a rapid thaw, melted by her fiery fury, 'Well, keep your phone calls, Tremaine!' she exploded hotly. 'I don't need you ringing up to gloat or...'

'Gloat?'

Feeling she could cheerfully kill him for that phony note of surprise in his voice, Pernelle didn't deign to take him up on that. 'So, in case you haven't got the message,' she hurled, enraged, sarcastic, 'I don't need you ringing—*ever*!'

'Don't hold your breath!' he snarled before she'd barely finished—then bang, his phone went down.

The swine, how dared he hang up on her, she fumed, and had the hardest work in the world not to burst into tears. She wouldn't cry, though, she wouldn't. He wasn't worth her tears, he just wasn't. The swine, the rotten heartbreaking, womanising swine!

It was perhaps as well that things were very quiet at the office just now, she reflected when she got back to Primrose Cottage that night, for her day had not been very productive.

Hunter was still everywhere with her that early evening, and she recalled his phone call over and over again. Not that there was much to go over, the lying tyke! Of course he'd rung up to gloat! Since he'd definitely stated that he hadn't called to speak to Mike, his call had to be a '*now* ask me about my decision about lending your employer some money' rubbing-it-in kind of call.

She recalled that moment when she'd asked if he had made his decision about Mike—and what had made her ask the question. Then she found a degree of comfort in the fact that if Hunter ever thought she'd an atom of caring for him—then, with luck, her attitude today should have made him think differently.

Any small comfort from that thought, however, dwindled the more the evening went on, and then Pernelle found she could no longer sustain her fury with him. And that was something which she had instinctively been dreading. For when the fury died down it allowed space for other emotion. Other raw and painful emotion, and the hurt began to bite.

The hound, she tried to whip up anger against him, and even made herself think of the females who'd trotted up his path on a Saturday morning and not left until the afternoon. She made herself think of Lily, the most recent of them all so far as she could judge—but that made the pain worse, not better.

When Pernelle realised she was actually standing listening for the sounds of his car—when he had never come down to Myrtle Cottage on a Tuesday, so far as she knew—she despaired of ever getting him out of her head.

When, as it neared nine o'clock, she suddenly found she was questioning whether she had been wrong to treat him so icily when he'd telephoned, she began to wonder if she was right in the head! The papers were always full of women who, no matter how despicable the men they loved, still insisted on seeing them as Mr Wonderful. But she'd read that letter from Hunter—countless times—so she *couldn't* be wrong, and there was certainly nothing 'Mr Wonderful' about that!

Just then, when Pernelle was losing all hope of breaking away from constantly thinking of Hunter, her phone rang. Crazily, she thought for a moment that it was him—and then she remembered the way he had slammed the phone down on her just after lunch. There had been something very final about that!

'Oh, you're in!' her mother exclaimed, as soon as she answered the phone. 'I was afraid you'd be out,' and Pernelle was glad to have something else on which to pin her thoughts.

'You sound worried! What's the trouble?' she asked quickly.

'There's no trouble, but I am a bit concerned about something,' her mother replied, and went on to tell her how Bruce's twin was still poorly and that Bruce had started to be anxious about her and wanted to go to Cornwall to see her. The problem was that he didn't want to go without his wife.

'But you don't want to go?' Pernelle asked, having always thought her mother had got on quite well with her sister-in-law.

'It isn't that I don't *want* to go, but that I *can't*!'

'Why not?' Pernelle queried.

'Arthur!'

'Arthur?'

'You've forgotten, I'm looking after Mrs Deakin's dog,' and as Pernelle was recalling how Mrs Deakin was in hospital and how Arthur objected to being anywhere but his own neighbourhood, her mother was going on, 'And Beryl is highly allergic to dog fur. She just doesn't need red watery eyes and the sneezes added to the rest of her problems.'

'I see,' Pernelle replied, and, since her parent wouldn't have rung to tell her all this without some purpose, she searched and realised, 'Ah, you want me to have Arthur! I'll have to leave him in during the day, but I could come home in my lunch hour and let him...'

'Actually, dear...' her mother began.

'You don't want me to look after him?'

'I do, but not there—here.'

'There?' Pernelle questioned.

'Mrs Deakin would worry herself silly if I farmed him out anywhere. Can you?'

'When do you want me to come?'

'As soon as possible. It'll only be for a day or two,' her mother persuaded. 'Bruce, as you know, is very close to his sister, so as soon as he's settled in his mind that she'll be all right we can return to Yeovil. Having Arthur couldn't have happened at a worse time, but I just can't send him back to the kennels—Mrs Deakin would break her heart.'

'Can you leave it with me, Mum? I'll ring you back when I've got something sorted out,' Pernelle promised, and rang off.

Only a few seconds afterwards and she was having to push all thoughts of Hunter from her mind. Then she caught herself looking out of her sitting-room window as though hoping to see his car. And what with her constant listening for him and looking for him all the while, it seemed to Pernelle then that it might not be a bad idea if she went away for a few days.

She went back to the phone and dialled Mike Yolland's home number. 'How are you, Pernelle?' Mike's wife answered her call. 'It seems ages since we saw each other.'

'I'm fine,' Pernelle told her, then after a few more pleasantries, she went on, 'Something's come up, and I wanted to ask Mike if I could have a few days off at short notice.'

'If it's only for a few days, I could cover for you,' Zena offered, and confided, 'To be honest, I wouldn't mind being near to where Mike is for a day or two. He's a bit down at the moment, as you probably know.' Then, 'Hang on, I'll get him, he's upstairs giving Tom ten good reasons why he should stop messing about and go to sleep.' And before Pernelle could tell her not to, that she would ring back when it was more convenient, she had gone, and the next voice Pernelle heard was Mike's.

'Zena tells me you want time off,' he greeted her, and Pernelle launched into the Arthur situation, to have Mike respond, 'You've had hardly any time off this year,' and follow on to suggest that she took the rest of the week off. 'Will that be long enough?' he asked.

'I'm sure it will be. Thanks, Mike,' she added, and ended the call to ring her mother while she still had the phone in her hand and to tell her that she could be there tomorrow.

'Tomorrow? Why, that's super!' her mother replied in delighted surprise. 'What time can you get here?' she wanted to know, and Pernelle realised that the sooner she got to Yeovil, the sooner her mother and Bruce could get to Cornwall, where Bruce could satisfy himself about his sister's health.

'If I leave here early, I could be with you around nine,' she promised, and, with her mother much relieved, Pernelle went to pack a case—Hunter in her thoughts the whole while.

After another terrible night, Pernelle was up early the following morning, and had given up trying to oust Hunter from her thoughts. She had locked up her cottage, though, and was reversing her car down her drive when she looked back at her property and suddenly realised that everything she loved about the place had faded under the unhappiness of being in love with Hunter.

She had barely started on her journey when the thought suddenly occurred to her of how unbearable future weekends were going to be, loving Hunter, hating Hunter—and having her emotions over him torn apart.

She arrived at her mother's home before nine, and was generally fussed over by her, and by Bruce—and by Arthur. 'He remembers you,' Bruce suggested when Arthur jumped up, tail wagging frantically, as he placed his front paws on her legs and barked.

'He hides at the mere whisper of the words "Dog obedience classes",' her mother confided drily. 'Now, I've got breakfast all ready for you.'

'I've eaten,' Pernelle fibbed, off her food and more concerned that her mother should get on her way.

Ten minutes after her mother and Bruce had driven off, Pernelle took Arthur for a long walk. She walked him again in the afternoon, and in the evening she went to the hospital and visited Mrs Deakin—but the whole time the realisation of what she must do was coming, with certain inevitability, closer and closer.

She returned to her mother's home after her hospital visiting, with Hunter as ever in her head, and to dwell more and more on the women in his life. More and more on the women who turned up at his weekend cottage—and who spent hours in there with him.

Pernelle went up to bed growing very much aware that she couldn't take it—this constant turning of the knife, the jealousy, the despair. She dropped off into a fitful sleep, but was wide awake at three o'clock—the realisation of what she must do staring her in the face.

Her mother had been of the view that Hunter would not keep Myrtle Cottage for long, and would be selling up in no time. But, with a clarity born from the pain of despair, Pernelle realised that, since he showed no signs of leaving, she must be the one to go.

Her first thought on waking on Thursday morning, however, was that no, she couldn't possibly cut off all chance of seeing Hunter. But, when hard on the heels of that thought jealousy started to nip when she thought of the attractive women who pulled up in their cars, she began to waver.

The matter was settled without further argument, however, when Pernelle recalled her fear that she had given away how deeply she cared for him. Pride, if nothing else, then screamed that she should not sit passively waiting for a day to come when she might do something—who knew what—which would confirm for him that love him indeed she did. While it seemed unlikely after their snarled conversation yesterday that they would ever speak to each other again, Pernelle still felt panicky. Who knew that should they at some future weekend break their silence—be it about sheep or whatever—she might, with a tongue that seemed to have a will of its own when Hunter was about, reveal, while striving to keep it hidden, how she felt about him. He could make her angry enough to make her tongue unwary, she knew that.

That thought, coupled with the memory of how astute he was, was sufficient to make her impatient for nine o'clock when she could ring the estate agents in East Durnley. She could take anything, she realised, but that Hunter should know she was in love with him.

When she did speak with Rufus Sayer about selling Primrose Cottage, he was all for coming to see her that morning. 'I'm not at home, I'm away for a few days,' she told him hurriedly—and heard that that was no problem.

'I'll still have details somewhere from when you bought it,' he stated. 'So unless you've been knocking walls out the room sizes will be the same.'

'I've redecorated, but that's all,' Pernelle replied, ignoring a weaker self that was having last-minute doubts. 'So if you could put the property on your books as soon as possible, I'll give you a ring about viewing arrangements as soon as I get back.'

'Leave it to me, Miss Richards,' he said warmly, clearly having remembered her. 'Consider Primrose Cottage on our books as of now.'

Pernelle put the phone down after her call and didn't feel in the least better for having done what she had. She spent that day walking Arthur and trying to keep busy while telling herself the whole while that, drastic though her action now seemed to her, if she was to save herself from more heartache, it was the only action she could have taken.

She lay awake in her bed that long night, and had never ever experienced such loneliness of spirit as she endured then. She was up early walking Arthur, and got back to have her mother telephone.

'I rang you several times yesterday,' Stella Lewis told her. 'Do I suspect Arthur has been having some bonus walkies?'

'I'm trying to walk some of his energy off him,' Pernelle replied.

'Impossible,' her mother declared. 'Bruce tried that and it didn't work.' She then went on to say that Beryl appeared much improved and that Bruce, his anxieties lessened, was ready to return to Yeovil tomorrow. 'We should be with you about lunchtime,' she ended.

'I'll have a meal ready,' Pernelle replied, and spent the day giving Arthur, who had quickly wormed his way into her affections, a lot of attention.

Since his mistress seemed short on visitors, Pernelle visited Mrs Deakin for an hour in the afternoon, and assured her that, though missing her, Arthur was in splendid form.

Pernelle was up early on Saturday morning, her thoughts instantly with Hunter and how he was probably having a lie-in—wherever he was. Jealousy tried to take hold, but she chased around finding jobs to do, and again took Arthur for a walk.

Her mother and Bruce arrived at about twelve-thirty and, while several times it was on the tip of Pernelle's tongue to tell them of her decision to sell Primrose Cottage, she found she could not. They would naturally want to know what had brought her to this decision, she realised, just as she realised that the ache in her heart about Hunter was too raw a wound for her to be able to tell even her mother—as close as they had always been.

'You'll stay until tomorrow, of course,' her mother stated, as they tucked into Bruce's favourite bread and butter pudding.

'I . . .' Pernelle opened her mouth to agree, but was overcome by a feeling of restlessness. 'Do you mind if I don't?' she asked lightly, and remembered half a dozen chores she wanted to do before Monday.

She left Yeovil at a little after two, and a return of the loneliness of spirit she had experienced last night attached itself to the restlessness she was feeling. She knew she had done right to put Primrose Cottage on the market, yet at the same time she was having heartaching second thoughts about leaving.

She stopped off in East Durnley to do some bits of shopping she had been too woolly-headed to think of yesterday. Then she started on the last lap of her journey with the treacherous thought starting to take hold that until she had actually agreed to sell her cottage to someone, she still had time to change her mind.

Realising that she was being pathetically weak, Pernelle drove through Chumleigh Edge knowing that it was the throwing away of any chance to see Hunter at the weekends that was at the back of her wavering. Don't be ridiculous! she pulled herself up smartly. After the icy and sarcastic way she'd spoken to him on the phone she'd be lucky if he so much as acknowledged her existence ever again, much less speak to her ever again.

It was with something of a jolt that the first thing she saw as she slowed down on approaching her cottage was the For Sale sign which was planted in her garden. Somehow she hadn't expected a notice to be erected quite so soon. But since it was standard practice and since Rufus Sayer had only been acting on her instructions she swallowed down the emotion seeing the sign caused her and went through the routine of opening her gates.

Hunter's car was nowhere to be seen, she noted as she drove her car on to its standing area. Nor was there any other car about. Perhaps this one's come on foot, she thought—and had never felt so down.

She felt even more down at the thought that followed. The thought that perhaps Hunter wasn't here. Perhaps he wasn't coming this weekend! Oh, heavens, she grieved as she got out of her car, here she was devastated that she wouldn't have a sight of him this weekend—how the dickens was she going to feel when, by her own doing, she had given up all chance of seeing him ever again?

With her case on the gravel beside her she turned back to her car and inserted the key in the car door lock, then heard a sound—and froze. That was Hunter's front door!

She purposely kept her back turned. By her reckoning it was somewhere around four-thirty. If this was some other female on her way out—after lord knew how many hours—then she just didn't want to know.

But Pernelle very soon discovered that she was going to have to know, because to her ears those footsteps weren't going down Hunter's drive! But if her hearing—along with the flurry of her heartbeats—hadn't gone totally haywire, those footsteps were crossing the front of Hunter's property—and crossing over on to hers!

She wanted to swallow, but couldn't. Wanted to turn, but couldn't. Then, realising those footsteps sounded not female at all but a most masculine firm tread, she discovered that, far from not acknowledging her, far from not so much as speaking to her ever again, Hunter was addressing her back and was absolutely furious as well as vocal as he roared, 'Just where the blue blazes have you been?'

Refusing to swallow, refusing to crumple, Pernelle took a grip on herself—then turned round. She was not

mistaken, she saw, as she looked up into his smoulder-
ing dark eyes. He *was* furious!

But nobody roared at her like that. 'It's got nothing
to do with you where I've been!' she roused herself to
slam back at him—that, or go under. With that she raised
her chin an uppity inch or so. But, just as she was going
to order him off her land he, ignoring her reply completely, got in first.

'And just *what*—is *that* all about?' he rapped, pointing
an enraged finger at her For Sale notice.

Pernelle took her eyes from him to glance at the sign,
then back again. But just to look at him made her heart
pound, made her weak, so that it took all she had to
coolly survey him, and to find yet more hauteur to
answer arrogantly, 'I'd have thought the sign self-
explanatory.'

Oh, help, she thought when immediately a glint of
pure steel entered his eyes—he wasn't at all enamoured
by her tone.

Though she couldn't have said she was all that
enamoured by his tone either when he thundered, 'The
devil it is!' and beat her arrogance into a cocked hat
when he demanded, 'What the hell's going on?'—and
sounded for all the world as if he thought he had every
right to know!

CHAPTER NINE

THERE was no answer to Hunter's furious 'What the hell's going on?', Pernelle decided. Well, not unless she forgot all pride and confessed that she couldn't take the jealousy that gnawed away at her about his women, but that, more particularly, she was heart and soul in love with him.

Since there was no way he was going to know anything of the sort from her lips, however, that left her with only one option. She put her head in the air and went sailing over to her front door. She was feeling so shaken, though, that she was more than glad she'd attached a door-key to her car key-ring—she knew she'd be fumbling forever in her bag for her key were it not right there in her hand.

But had she nursed any idea that if she just walked away from Hunter—his question unanswered—that was the end of the matter, it didn't take long for her to find out differently. For, as she opened her front door, stepped inside her sitting-room and went to close the door after her, so she discovered that Hunter, his fury in no way abated by her uppity treatment, was right there with her—wedging her suitcase in the doorway!

'Don't you want this?' he gritted, and, startled, Pernelle begun to seriously dislike him for so easily making her feel a fool for having forgotten it.

Indeed, she was so worked up, she had forgotten her shopping too, but she'd go and bring that in later. 'Thank...' she began, but broke off when, ignoring the hand she'd stretched out for her case, he used the case as a battering ram to push his way into her sitting-room. 'Thank you,' she insisted, when he set it down on her carpet.

When he straightened up, though, she quailed inwardly at the unswerving no-nonsense fierceness in the dark eyes that burned into hers. And that was before he barked harshly, 'Just that—and that's it?'

Again she wanted to swallow—but she would not! 'You want a tip?' she questioned insolently, and half wished she hadn't when she saw his hands clench. Then he took a deep breath as if striving for control, then used one of his hands—to push her easily locked front door fast to.

'Cut the sauce!' he gritted, and Pernelle fought desperately to find some strength, but she felt isolated with him in her sitting-room, and could barely think clearly.

'Huh!' she scoffed. 'What kind of answer would you like me to make? The last time I was in conversation with you,' she raced on before he could tell her, 'you slammed the phone down on me!'

'I should stay talking after what you said?' he challenged. And Pernelle damned her brain, and damned him too, that when she had since gone over her conversation with him a dozen times or more, she didn't understand what he was referring to.

Which left her no alternative but to skirt round him to the door. 'This place isn't big enough for both of us,' she told him waspishly, and, raising her hand to the door-latch, she turned it.

She did not manage to open it very far, however, for suddenly the flat of Hunter's right hand was against the door and he was pushing it to again. She darted him a swift look and saw that he was looking at her with a considering look in his eyes, and she panicked again when, some of his fury subsided, he questioned deliberately, 'You're saying that your decision to sell has something to do with me?'

In her view Hunter Tremaine was too clever by half, but in acknowledging that she had walked straight into that one, Pernelle endeavoured to keep her panic from showing. 'Hmm!' she shrugged, to let him know he was wide of the mark, but a yard or so from her was much too close, so she came away from the door—and thought it best, since he clearly wasn't going to be moved before he was ready, to change tack. 'So what did I say that was so very dreadful that you should hang up on me?' she challenged, the idea of taking the battle into his camp a splendid decoy, she thought. Even if she was suddenly more than a little confused to know what the battle was about—other than that she was fighting to guard the secret of her love.

For an age, or so it seemed to her, Hunter just stood and stared levelly down at her. Then, just as if he had never forgotten a word of that conversation either, 'Apart from caustically letting me know you didn't need me ringing you *ever*, you had the astounding audacity to accuse me of ringing up to *gloat*!' he reminded her, and while her eyes were growing wide as she realised that he was doing it again—making *her* feel the guilty one— his nerve was endless— 'Ye gods,' he added with a touch of his old aggression, 'I could have throttled you for——'

'Now just a minute!' Pernelle roused herself to cut him off. 'I may be dumb, Tremaine, but I'm not so dumb that I can't clearly remember the letter you wrote to Mike—after as good as hinting that the loan was his— stating that you'd turned him down! I'm supposed to...'

'You took that letter personally? As being against you?' he sliced in to ask, causing Pernelle to see, too late, that she hadn't underestimated him when she'd labelled him astute.

'N-no, of course not!' she denied, panicking afresh. 'I . . .' But, floundering, she was glad when this time, his eyes steady on hers, Hunter cut in again.

'Perhaps it might relieve your mind to know that it was with you in mind that I wrote that first encouraging letter,' he stated.

'Much good did it do him!' Pernelle flew, gaining her second wind. 'So, from the first, you *were* just trying to get at me through . . .'

'Confound it, woman!' Hunter suddenly bellowed. Then, looking aggravatedly at her, 'Hell's teeth, was there ever such a female for getting hold of the wrong end of it?'

'I knew *you* couldn't possibly be in the wrong! That it would all . . .'

'Will you shut up!' he chopped her off thunderously, and when, momentarily silenced, she stared hostilely at his exasperated expression, 'Just shut up and listen,' he ordered crisply.

Several snappy answers sprang to her lips, but, having been so rudely bellowed at, she settled for, 'This had better be good,' and stood woodenly waiting for him to go on.

'You wouldn't rather sit down?' he suggested.

That sounded rather as though he thought she might fall down—that, or he wasn't planning to leave in a hurry. 'No, I wouldn't!' she told him bluntly. To sit down and give her shaky legs a treat suddenly seemed a splendid idea—but too late now.

'Very well,' he accepted, and, looking her straight in the eyes, 'I rang on Tuesday to——'

'Not to apologise to Mike!'

'Are you going to shut up?'

'Go on.'

'I've nothing to *apologise* for!' Pernelle so nearly exclaimed *'Huh!'* again, but at his sharp acid look she changed her mind, and he waited no longer, but continued, 'Seeing that there were two letters, not one...'

'Two...?' Pernelle clamped her lips tightly closed at the 'I'm warning you' look he tossed at her.

'The only thing I'm sorry about is that, although both letters were posted at the same time, they didn't, for some reason, arrive at the same time. I realised that at once, of course, from the frigid way you spoke once you knew it was me on the phone. But since——'

'Hang on a moment,' Pernelle cut in, 'I'm missing something here! What two letters are you talking about? Mike received one addressed to him on Tuesday, but...'

'They were both addressed to him. The one, as you know from Braddon Consolidated in which I set out my reasons for being unable to risk company funds to help him out.'

'And the other?' Pernelle questioned, her anger suddenly gone, her attention glued on Hunter.

'The other,' he replied, 'the one which arrived on Wednesday, was a letter personally from me, in which I made a few tightening-up suggestions at business level, and at the same time offered the finance he requires from my own resources.'

Pernelle's mouth fell open with shock, and for several seconds she wasn't thinking but was just staring at Hunter dumbstruck. 'Y-you—he...' she managed, and swallowed hard. The money Mike wanted was a small fortune, and yet Hunter—with a hint that she personally had something to do with it—had offered to advance such a sum out of his own funds! 'Oh, Hunter,' she said and, whether he thought her a contrary female or not, she just had to go and sit down.

'May I?' he enquired evenly, and she glanced at him to see that he had come over to the settee too, and was waiting for permission to be seated.

'Of course,' she replied, her tone very different from what it had been, as she moved up to one end of the settee and made room for him at the other. Then, her head clearer, and with room for a couple of people on the settee in between them, 'Can you tell me again—slowly?' she requested, and felt her heart lurch when, for the first time since she had turned round by her car and looked at him, his mouth picked up a little at the corners.

'There's not a lot to tell...' He hesitated. 'Or,' he seemed to deliberate again, she thought, 'or maybe there is,' he added, somewhat obscurely. 'Anyhow—my decision made, I rang on Tuesday to speak to you, and...'

'The parcel!' she exclaimed out of the blue. 'You rang about the parcel you were expecting.'

'Er...' he murmured, but left it there, to resume, 'I rang, and soon knew, from your tone as much as anything, that only one letter had reached Yolland.'

'You rang him to check?'

'I rang to speak to you,' Hunter corrected. 'Until then it had never occurred to me, although perhaps it should have done, that the letters wouldn't arrive together. As far as I was concerned there was no need for me to ring him—though it was quite possible that he would ring me.'

From what Pernelle knew of Mike she thought he would be so overjoyed at Hunter's personal letter and offer that it was a *certainty* that he would telephone. 'He did, didn't he? Ring, I mean,' she questioned, her heart beating crazily within her at the thought that Hunter was anything but the swine her head would try to have her believe.

'He rang while I was at a meeting,' he replied, causing her to think it was no wonder that he had come down to Chumleigh Edge for a break. Since Mike would have rung him straight away, Hunter's meeting must have been one of those breakfast meetings that, as yet, hadn't arrived in East Durnley. 'My PA gave me the message when I got back to say that "over the moon" was an understatement for Yolland's reaction.'

Oh, Hunter, Pernelle thought, and wanted to beg his forgiveness for that word 'gloat'. But, 'Poor Mike,' she said instead. 'He's had a terribly worrying time of it.'

'He's not the only one!' Hunter retorted sharply, causing Pernelle to think shakenly that he didn't care very much that all her sympathies were for her employer.

Which they were not. If Hunter was in trouble, then even though she couldn't see what trouble he could be in, because it was obvious that he had no money worries, she wanted to do all she could to help. 'You—you're worried too—are worrying?' she asked urgently.

'I've not been—easy in my head for some while now,' he replied before she could offer to help, whatever his problem might be. But then he had her turning in her seat to look at him in surprise when he added, 'Your freezing attitude on the phone last Tuesday didn't help matters.' Again there seemed to be something very deliberate about what he was saying—just as if he was choosing his words very carefully.

'I'm—not sure I understand,' she replied slowly.

She was still trying to work out how her cold attitude on the phone could have any effect on his business worries, when he went on, 'Don't you see that with any other woman, I wouldn't have given a damn?'

Her throat went bone dry again. She wanted to swallow, but dared not. Idiot, she scolded. Hunter wasn't meaning her as Pernelle Richards, but her as his weekend neighbour, or her as Mike Yolland's secretary—but even then she couldn't make sense of it. Which left her still floundering, and having to ask, 'You—er—wouldn't?'

'I would *not*!' he stated categorically. 'But that *you* should believe I could act the way you accused. That you should believe I'd ring up to *gloat*! Confound it,' he muttered grimly, 'was it any wonder I should be furious with you?'

'I—er...' she tried, but didn't get very far. Furious! He'd been boiling, she recalled—and just had to ask, 'W-why?'

Hunter was already turned in his seat, was already looking at her—indeed, his dark eyes seemed to be searching into her very soul for something. Then, 'Can't you guess?' he asked very quietly—and Pernelle's heartbeats went haywire again.

She was still trying to cope with stunned brain messages which were belatedly working out that, from what he'd said about not giving a damn had it been any other woman, he must mean he valued her good opinion—above all others! From which the only guess she could come up with was that Hunter, therefore, might in some small way care for her! Immediately Pernelle discounted the idea. It was not to be, so she must not go nursing ridiculous ideas.

She had flicked her glance away from him, but, having realised that any notion that Hunter might care for her was too far-fetched to be true, she glanced back at him—and saw that, somehow appearing extremely tense suddenly, he was looking at her expectantly for her answer.

But, 'I'm—er—not very good at guessing games,' was the only answer she could find for him.

He looked a little disappointed, she thought, as he enquired, 'I'm to go the long way round?'

Long or short, she was beginning to feel a mass of agitation inside. Though, since her brain seemed to need all the help it could get, even her instincts deserting her, she didn't think she'd make much of a job of analysing a shortened version of whatever it was Hunter had to say. 'It—um—might be a good idea,' she replied, and knew more agitation when, after looking into her eyes for long, long moments, Hunter, while still keeping some space between them, moved a little nearer.

Then, with what seemed to her to be a steadying breath, 'So be it,' he said, and then, to her amazement, opened up, 'To go back to the very beginning—it was at the tail end of last year that, while I was still enjoying the cut and thrust of business, still enjoying working hard, enjoying to the full living and working in London, I suddenly found I was examining more and more frequently the quality of my life.'

'Quality?' Pernelle questioned, recovering fast from her surprise that Hunter was opening up the way he was, and feeling quite overjoyed herself that while in the past they'd touched on plenty of topics, this was the first time he'd let her into anything closer, more personal to him.

'Something, I wasn't sure what, seemed to be missing in my life,' he replied. 'Having achieved most of my goals in business, I felt there was nothing I was missing there, so I concluded that perhaps I should investigate a different lifestyle.'

'Which is why you bought Myrtle Cottage?' Pernelle questioned, thankful that her brain wasn't as half asleep as she had supposed. It had worked that bit out, anyhow.

Hunter favoured her with a pleasant look that made her feel all soft inside about him and cancelled out any ridiculous notion that she had ever seriously disliked him, and answered, 'It seemed a good idea to take a small place in the country—nothing large or imposing. I've worked hard all my life, more often than not seven days a week, so I only meant to sample an alternative lifestyle, not being at all sure how I'd take to too much serenity after a lifetime of going at it full stretch.' He paused, then added quietly, 'So, having found my small place, in quite an idyllic spot, and having engaged a builder to carry out such alterations as I deemed essential, what did I find but that some quite stunning female—who I knew I'd never met—had pulled up at my gates and was belligerently charging me "Going to ruin it, Tremaine?" and accusing me of cheating her out of Myrtle Cottage into the bargain.'

Pernelle was still lodged somewhere in that blissful 'quite stunning female', but fought hard to get her mind away from that heart-warming compliment. 'I'm—er—sorry about that. It was unfair, but, until you came along, my bid for Myrtle Cottage had been accepted.'

'So I discovered,' Hunter smiled.

'You didn't know until then?'

'My solicitors dealt with everything once I'd seen the property. After that Saturday I met you, though, I made a few enquiries.' He looked thoughtfully at her, then went on, 'As a matter of fact you almost lost Primrose Cottage in the same way.'

'I did?' she exclaimed, her eyes shooting wide.

'But you didn't,' he answered. 'I was abroad when Primrose Cottage came on the market. As soon as I got back and found out about it, I played with the idea of buying it and turning the two places into one.'

'You'd have converted the properties back to the way they used to be?'

'It was the obvious thing to do, both from a living point of view and, businesswise—should I find my country weekends tedious—from a re-selling point of view.'

Pernelle could see that. 'So you rang the estate agents?'

He nodded. 'And was informed that Primrose Cottage was still open to offer. But,' he regarded her steadily for a moment before continuing, 'just as I was about to make arrangements to look over it, I suddenly found I was asking if anyone else was interested in it.'

'He told you I was?' she queried.

Hunter gave her a rueful look. 'Can you imagine how shaken I felt, with making decisions and "going for it" second nature to me, when the estate agent only had to state that a Miss Pernelle Richards had put in a bid, and I—to my immense surprise—found I was backing off?'

'Good heavens!' Pernelle exclaimed chokily, somehow knowing that up till then Hunter had never backed off in his life.

For a few moments more he surveyed her quietly, and then, to cause her heartbeats to race again, 'Then you moved in and my troubles really began—and my weekends didn't get a chance to be tedious.'

'Troubles? Er—they didn't?' she choked, but just in time she realised she was taking his remarks far too personally, so she hurriedly added, 'Oh, of course, you mean the noise, the...'

'I mean you generally, Pernelle Richards,' he cut in, his expression serious, his eyes never leaving her face.

'Me—generally?' she questioned, and had the hardest work in the world not to swallow. 'H-how?' she stammered as nerves began to attack.

'How?' He shook his head. 'That's a question I've been asking myself for weeks now. What was it about this long-legged female with the alluring lips that plagued me from the start?'

'Pl-plagued?'

'There's no other word for it. A side issue was your paper-stripping performances, which through my wall sounded as though you had a whole troupe of wall-of-death riders doing a continuous circuit.'

'Oh,' she murmured, her heartbeats settling down to a dull routine. 'I'm afraid it was necessary—it had to be done.'

'Of course it had,' he agreed, and made her feel like jelly inside as he added, 'And despite the fact that the first Sunday I was down after you'd moved in I was forced, by your racket, to leave for London early, I've admired you tremendously for tackling the redecorations all by yourself.'

Oh, don't, Hunter, she wanted to tell him, basking in his compliment, but still weakened by it. 'Mr Johns did the rewiring,' she thought to mention, but added, 'I'm sorry you had to leave earlier than you'd meant to.'

'Think nothing of it,' he replied pleasantly. 'There were other times when, on account of you, I delayed my departure.' And, while Pernelle's emotions hopped on a merry-go-round again, 'Times too when I arrived much earlier than I would have, had you not been here.'

Pernelle swallowed, then took a shaky breath. 'On—account of me, do you mean?' She swallowed again, when he moved closer still, as though to read what he could in her melting brown eyes.

'Believe it,' he replied.

'W-why?' she had to ask.

'A question I asked myself countless times when I couldn't understand why myself. Any more than I could get to grips with why it should irk me to see you getting into some man's car, or why I should ponder the rest of the evening, were you going steady?'

Oh, dear heaven, what was he saying? Pernelle panicked—that he was interested in her? Don't be ridiculous, said her head. But the question wouldn't go away. Though since it wasn't a question she could ask—not unless she wanted to risk the humiliation of him rolling about the floor convulsed with laughter—the only other thing she could think of to say was, 'Was that the Saturday I said "Good evening" to you—and you ignored me?'

'I can't be perfect all the time,' he murmured drily, and all at once the tension she was feeling suddenly evaporated and she burst out laughing. Her laughter subsided, though, when, struck by the seriousness of his expression, she definitely heard him breathe, 'Oh, you're so lovely.'

'Hunter.' She said his name, and it fell involuntarily from her lips. But no sooner was the softly spoken sound out than, at the alert look that came to his eyes, as if he suspected how emotional she felt about him at just that moment, she fought desperately for something hard, trite, anything that would make him think differently.

But, just as if he knew about that too, he commanded her suddenly, 'Don't! Just relax, Pernelle.' And while her lips parted and she drew another shaky breath, 'I swear I won't hurt you,' he promised.

Hunter, you don't know, she wanted to tell him. You don't know the power that you do have to hurt me. But, as she stared at him, large-eyed, while trying to hide how very afraid she was that, whatever all this was about, she was going to end up hurting—and hurting like the very devil—Hunter suddenly moved the rest of the way near to her, and gently bent his head and touched his lips to her parted mouth.

'Trust me,' he said.

'Why?' she asked—and nearly collapsed at his reply.

'Because I love you,' he answered, oh, so quietly.

'You love me?' she questioned, stunned, disbelieving.

'I do.'

'Since when?' She'd meant it to come out scornful, scoffing, but she wanted so much to believe him that that was how her question came out—serious, and wanting seriously, genuinely to know.

'Although I've only recently acknowledged myself what has kept me sleepless, appetiteless, angry, glad; what has been responsible for all my swings of mood; it seems to me now that I've always loved you,' he answered her question in the same serious vein, his eyes fixed solely on hers.

'Always?' she asked chokily, realising, as she remembered the sharp acid way he'd been with her at the beginning, that she was right to disbelieve him.

But, 'Always,' he agreed firmly. 'Even while not accepting what was happening to me, I could find no explanation for why—as far back as five weeks ago—when that Sunday I was on the point of leaving for London, I should look out of the window and see you setting off perkily down the road. Suddenly then, when

I was about to lock up and go, it struck me that I shouldn't mind a walk myself—that I could leave for London in the morning if I wanted.'

Pernelle stared at him, needing help, wanting help, but there was none coming. This was the here and now, and it was so, so important, and she was in it on her own. 'You—followed me?' she questioned with what voice she had—then found she'd got it wrong—which didn't surprise her—when he shook his head.

'It was pure coincidence that, by another route, you arrived at the same barn I was sheltering in,' he replied.

'The cows!' she exclaimed. 'You...'

'I was a brute,' he accepted all blame. 'And you were so wonderful, so brave when, goaded by me, you faced your fear and walked past those cows.'

'You knew I was afraid,' she stated.

'You were terrified!' he corrected, and set her heart thundering anew when he took hold of one of her hands and added softly, 'Who could help but admire your guts at doing what you did?'

'Was that what you were doing when you came further away from that barn to watch me?' she asked, a trifle tartly, she had to own, as the scene came back to her. She had thought she hated him then.

'I came out of the barn not only to watch you,' he answered, 'but to be ready if you needed help.'

'Honestly?'

'Don't doubt it,' he answered her, but asked quickly, 'You were all right afterwards? You didn't suffer any repercussions?'

'I was fine,' she confessed. 'In actual fact,' she remembered, 'I felt rather elated afterwards. Though...' Abruptly she stopped.

'Though?' he prompted.

'Though—um—well, I—er—remember thinking at the time that the elation must be because I'd at last faced up to an old fear—a relic from childhood—but that it—um—could have nothing to do with you.'

'You were starting to feel for me?' he quickly took up.

Oh, heavens, Pernelle fretted—how could she have forgotten how astute he was? 'I thought it was hate,' she tried to kill the scent.

'But it wasn't?'

'I... I—didn't know then.'

'But you do now?'

'Oh, Hunter, you're making me nervous!' she cried in anguish.

'Oh, my love, don't fret, don't fret,' he said quickly, and suddenly he had one arm about her shoulders and was tenderly cradling her to him. 'I'm being unfair, aren't I, trying to make you say what I'm so urgently longing to hear, yet I haven't yet given you enough, explained enough—about my swings from friendly to furious—for you to trust me.' With that he bent to her hair and tenderly placed a featherlike kiss there—and for several seconds Pernelle just didn't know where she was.

But she had to wake her brain, had to try to think, impossible though she was finding that with Hunter's arm round her, with him kissing her hair—not to mention that, incredibly, she was sure she'd heard him say he loved her. Valiantly she struggled to keep her feet on terra firma, but with so much emotion chasing frantically about inside her it didn't surprise her that the question she found to ask was not to challenge his statement of love, but was a question about the morning after they had both sheltered in that barn.

'Would you really have left me stranded that Monday morning my car wouldn't start, had I not come and asked you for a lift?' she asked, and felt her love for Hunter course through her veins once more when—if he was expecting a question about trust, about love—he didn't so much as give her an askance look.

But, as though ready and willing to reply to anything that might trouble her, no matter how inconsequential it might seem, he looked down into her lovely brown eyes and replied, 'In all honesty, my dear, I don't know.' And, while she was still coping with that loving-sounding 'my dear', he was adding, 'What I do know is that I spent a work-filled week and that, although it was my practice, if I was going to come down, to arrive on a Saturday, I was being pulled to come down on Friday.'

'Pulled?'

'Without knowing it—by you.'

'Oh!' she exclaimed, and recalled swiftly, 'You *did* come down that Friday night!'

'You remember?'

'I—er—remember suddenly feeling—sort of more cheerful inside, after you arrived,' she confessed in a weak moment.

'Oh, Pernelle!' Hunter breathed softly. But just as his head started to come down, something else about that particular weekend returned to her, and suddenly she went icy cold inside. Abruptly she pulled back, and there was no mistaking, as the warmth went from her eyes, that she would not be receptive to his kisses. 'What's the matter?' he exclaimed, his expression swiftly altering. 'Have I got it all wrong?' he questioned urgently, and some of his colour seemed to drain from him. 'Oh, my h...' he began.

But Pernelle, her heart aching, was bluntly cutting him off. 'You don't love me!' she attacked tartly, and, discounting that he'd lost a scrap of colour, ready to discount everything he'd said, 'All you want is some sordid affair. Some...'

'Sordid affair? How *dare*...'

'Don't get on your high horse with me!' she yelled, refusing to listen to him as she pulled aggressively out of his hold. 'You must think I'm stupid as well as blind, not to have noticed the succession of women who roll up next door every Saturday...' She might have gone storming on, but suddenly she was arrested by the change in his expression, by the return of his colour—as though comprehension had just dawned.

'Oh, my lovely girl, you don't trust me yet, do you?' he questioned the moment he could get a word in. And quickly, before she could begin to erupt again, 'Those women you've seen calling, and staying for some long while some Saturdays—and if memory serves there were only two—were married ladies...'

'Huh!' she exploded, and would have shot to her feet, but, quick as a flash, Hunter grabbed both her hands and held her there.

'Married ladies, with young children,' he resumed, adding quickly, 'who also happen to be excellent secretaries glad of some Saturday work, since it meant that on that day their husbands were free to look after their children.'

Her mouth fell open slightly. 'Oh!' she whispered, and started to feel ashamed. 'They—were—er—um—temps?'

Hunter looked at her, now quiet again, now warm-eyed. 'You *will* trust me, I promise,' he assured her gently, and, towards that promise, he went on to explain in detail, 'When I set about investigating a new lifestyle,

I knew in advance that it was unlikely I'd spend my country weekends just idly twiddling my thumbs, so I had the end bedroom converted into a study. Somewhere around the time that you moved in I was playing with a business idea that needed some extra work putting in.' He broke off to smile gently at her and then went on, 'I'm used to working all hours, but thought to spare my PA. It was immaterial to me that, with Monday to Friday full, I should work weekends. But since it would mean that my PA wouldn't have to find time to type back any of the extra work, she was happy to find me a first-class Saturday secretary in East Durnley—Victoria Potter. When Victoria needed a Saturday free for a family wedding, she arranged to send a similarly situated secretarial friend along.'

'I—see,' Pernelle murmured, but even if her heart did feel so very much lighter, she felt dreadful at the same time for her accusations.

'Do you, my dear?' he asked quietly. 'Do you see that you were...' he paused, then his eyes fixed firmly, assessingly, on her eyes '...that you were—jealous—over nothing?' He waited, but, though she'd been racked by that demon jealousy, she knew it would be a real giveaway to admit it—to admit what he was looking for. From what she knew of Hunter, she wouldn't have been surprised had he snarled, 'To the devil with it!' and waited no longer and left her. But he did nothing of the sort. Instead, as though he understood the mass of panic, hope, and agitation she was inside, he offered, 'Perhaps it would help if I told you how that green-eyed monster has caused me to recognise that I have tendencies that border on the murderous.'

'You—you've been jealous?' she asked, startled.

'And then some,' he owned, though he qualified it with a wry smile that tilted her heart. 'Of course I wasn't acknowledging the emotion for what it was when I came home from a solitary dinner and saw you kissing your date in his car.'

'It—um—wasn't much of a kiss,' she saw no harm in revealing.

'Now she tells me! I had a lousy night and was glad to get out of bed the next morning.'

'That was the morning... I thought Mr Johns, the electrician, got you out of bed when he started banging about the place! You telephoned...'

'In point of fact, Pernelle, I'm always up at first light, earlier in winter,' Hunter butted in.

'But you rang to complain, and I thought...'

'I rang, while not understanding it myself then, because of a need I seemed to have developed to have some contact with you. To complain was an excellent excuse.'

'Honestly?' she queried, her eyes huge in her face.

He nodded, a love she was beginning to believe in showing in his eyes, as he went on, 'It was from that same need that I rang you at your office a couple of days later, making believe I'd rung up to speak to Yolland.'

Her eyes went saucer-wide. 'No!' she gasped, then, a smile starting somewhere deep inside her, 'You terrified me when you told me who you were.'

'You deserved it,' he laughed, 'speaking to me like that!'

'I—er—never expected the *chairman* of Braddon Consolidated to ring personally.'

'In normal times, he wouldn't have,' Hunter answered. 'But these weren't normal times. May I?' he questioned, and put his arm back round her shoulder where, as

Pernelle found it most comfortable, she did not shrug away, which Hunter took for consent, then backtracked to reveal more about his work. 'Because I like to keep up to date with what's happening elsewhere in the organisation I periodically have a batch of applications brought to me—which is how Yolland's application came to my notice. I'd gone by his factory many times on my way to the motorway, so the fact that he seemed in financial trouble stuck in my mind. Then I discovered that you were his secretary and when, in normal times, someone else would have written to him, I found that not only was I ringing you but, when I started to wonder what the hell I was doing—I was asking for him. Then, before I knew it, I was turning up at your place of work and, for the pure hell of it, insisting that you show me round. Then——' he broke off to rest his eyes on her '—I found I was enjoying just looking at you.'

Pernelle's heart raced, but all she could think of to say was a smiling, 'You—wretch!'

'True,' he smiled back. 'Though I got my come-uppance, my dear, when, after I'd happily delayed you sufficiently that Wednesday to make you give up your date for that evening, you damn well made me green with jealousy again by making a date for the next night.'

'Oh, Hunter!' she said helplessly.

He seemed to like the soft and gentle sound of his name on her lips. 'Love me a little—a tiny bit?' he asked.

She swallowed. 'A—a tiny bit,' she admitted, and as his arm tightened at the back of her she thought he was going to pull her tight up against him.

But, save for planting a delicious kiss on the corner of the nearest eyebrow, he restrained himself. 'Where was I?' he asked gruffly.

'Um—you'd just been looking over the factory,' she somehow managed to recall.

'Ah, yes. I spent that night at Myrtle Cottage and—for my sins—had my vandal neighbour break my window the next morning.' Pernelle had to laugh, and he paused for a second or two just to look at her, then continued, 'By the time I'd got in through your bedroom window, I was feeling so good about just being near you, experiencing a feeling of somehow never wanting to leave you, that I just had to pause to take stock. By the time I had your front door open, I'd swung about and become a surly brute.'

'You were a bit of a grouch,' she admitted.

'Until you made me laugh; then I was kissing you, and I was all over the place. I, Miss Richards,' he informed her, 'had the devil's own work to let you go.'

'If it's—er—any consolation, I was positively staggered at the way I'd responded to you,' she confessed.

'Sweet love,' he murmured, his eyes gentle on her as he remembered how it had been, the way she had yielded to him. 'What chance then did I have of sticking to my firm intention of not coming down on Friday?'

'You arrived at four o'clock on Saturday morning,' she trotted out unwarily.

'You couldn't sleep either?' Hunter asked instantly.

'Er—couldn't you?'

'Cheeky,' he murmured at the way she'd bounced his question back at him. 'Sleep was impossible that Friday night,' he owned nevertheless. 'It was going on for two in the morning when I thought, to hell with it, and afterwards drove like the wind to be nearer to you.'

'I saw you in the shop in the village that Saturday afternoon,' she recalled without difficulty.

'And cut me dead!' There was nothing wrong with his total recall either, she realised.

'I'm—sorry,' she apologised. 'I'd seen your—er—replacement temp coming up your drive...'

'And were jealous!' Hunter finished for her; clearly that reason had never occurred to him. 'I thought seeing me had reminded you of your response to me on Thursday—and that you were regretting it.' He paused to plant a light kiss on her temple, then, while Pernelle was coping with the after-effects of that, he was going on to relate, 'So there was I, back home, wanting to see you, wanting to talk to you, but, having just been cut by you, determined that I was not about to come knocking on your door—when what did I see from my window but sheep?'

'You banged on my wall. You were furious about those sheep eating your——'

'I didn't give a damn about what they were eating, I was just delighted to see you—and trying to hide it.'

'Wretch, did I say?' she queried. 'You did a jolly good job!' Her heart turned cartwheels at his grin, and again she fought to keep her feet on the ground. 'I've no recollection at all of leaving that gate open,' she said sedately; closing gates was instinctive to her.

'You didn't,' Hunter surprised her by stating.

'I didn't. But you...'

'Are you going to forgive me because I knew all the time that you weren't the culprit?' he asked, and without managing to look too abject, explained, 'I'd gone to the village for an afternoon paper, but they weren't in yet, so Mrs Wilson offered to get the paper boy to drop one in. Since your gates were closed when I came back, it didn't take much to conclude that the paper boy had used your drive as a short cut to my front door.'

Pernelle stared at Hunter open-mouthed again. 'Substitute rogue for wretch!' she tried to say sternly, but she could not help but laugh.

She was not laughing, though, when Hunter went on to remind her how he'd watched her go out that night and had been all the while on the listen for her coming back—and had then heard her cry out.

'You were in so fast—and I was so pleased to see you,' she recalled, remembering how Chris Farmer had had more than a cup of coffee in mind when she had invited him in.

'I had the devil's own work controlling the rage that came over me when I saw you being held—and against your will. I've never experienced such murderous feelings! I later went to bed with my emotions about you in such a complex muddle, it was as though suddenly I was the unprotected one—the vulnerable one. Can you wonder that the next time I saw you I was like a bear with a sore head?'

'Oh, Hunter!' she whispered, and when he stared gently back at her, that love still there in his eyes, it took her some moments to get her thoughts together. 'You objected to my putting up a makeshift fence,' she somehow remembered.

'And how!' he replied with feeling. 'Even while I was fighting against feeling wide open where you're concerned, something subconscious in me was saying that it was enough that our two properties were partitioned without you erecting more barriers.'

'You were horrid!' she let him know with a smile, but had to tack on, 'But you did make amends when you came round that night to look at my decorating—even if in actual fact you only came round to ask me to take in your parcel.'

'A lie.'

'What?'

'A lie, sweet Pernelle. When only the previous evening I'd asked "Would I lie?" what did I find myself doing the very next evening but lying my head off by inventing an expected parcel?'

'You mean that I've hunted in your shed and everywhere else—*needlessly*?'

'I'm afraid so.'

'But—but why?'

'Our old enemy vulnerability again. I was starting to be besotted about you, yet I didn't want you to think there was more in my coming round than that I wanted you to take in a parcel.'

'You devious——'

'You can't accuse me of anything I haven't at last faced up to,' Hunter volunteered. 'Only the next morning I found myself hanging around in my garage—just on the offchance of seeing you, and, the moment I did, off I went, trying to make believe I was in something of a rush. Then I discovered, while still stubbornly not seeing what was the matter with me, that the "parcel" had come in very handy when my need to have some contact with you got the better of me.'

'You phoned,' she pointed out.

'Tuesday, Wednesday and Thursday,' he agreed. 'By Friday, though, I was fast realising that you were in my thoughts night and day and that, while I was thinking about you far, far more than I'd ever thought about any other woman, there was a new, nebulous kind of dimension added, which I found most unsettling.'

'Is that why you didn't phone or come down that night?'

'I knew by then that I was into something that was taking charge of me, so I was striving with all I had for some logical thinking.'

'Did your logical thinking—er—bring you anything?' she asked quietly.

'Nothing,' he owned, 'except the illogicality that, when I was longing to see you, I should refuse to drive down. That pull to see you, though, had grown so strong by Saturday,' he went on, 'that, having left my car on the drive and come round to the rear door as normal, I saw your kitchen window was open and was on my way to enquire about that infernal parcel before I could think.'

'Ooh!' she sighed, and felt sufficiently confident then to be able to confess, 'And I was so pleased to see you that I scalded my hand.'

'You were pleased to see me?' Hunter took up straight away. Shyly she nodded. 'Little love,' he murmured, his arm about her tightening momentarily. 'How's your hand now?' he asked.

'You kissed it better,' she laughed.

'That was some kiss!' he remembered, and revealed, 'I was never so charmed by such a response, nor so stunned at the way my heart was pounding. And while all I wanted to do when I let you go was to take you in my arms again, I was at the same time striving desperately to give myself sound reasons for not doing so.'

'You managed to find some?' she questioned with a laugh, her confidence increasing by the minute.

'The only thing I knew for certain, in the danger of that moment, was that I didn't want some brief affair,' he replied quietly, and, as her heart began to race anew, 'But I didn't know why.'

'You discovered why, later?' she asked huskily.

'Oh, yes, my sweet love,' he breathed. 'The very next night, in fact.'

'When you called to see if there were any messages—to see if your friend had called...'

'I wasn't expecting any friend to call,' Hunter confessed. 'I wanted to see you—and needed an excuse. Then before I knew it we were at each other's throats, ending up in each other's arms, and suddenly, like a great burst of light, I knew that what had been the matter with me all this time was that I was—am—heart and soul in love with you.'

For a few moments Pernelle just sat and stared, then, 'You knew then—that moment when you sat up and...'

'That's when I knew,' he confirmed. 'There was I, in shock, with my heart thundering to beat the band, with everything inside me going wild because could it be, going by your giving response, that you, my darling, darling girl, loved me in return? There was no one else in the world then except just you and me,' he murmured lovingly—then shook his head, to continue. 'But while I was high up there on cloud nine and just about to declare my love, what did I hear but you, as cool as you like, at this *most stupendous moment in my life*, dare, actually *dare*, to bring work into it!'

'Oh, I'm so sorry!' Pernelle exclaimed, horrified that she could have appeared so insensitive to him. 'You were furious.'

'I was,' he agreed. 'But I should be the one to apologise for my foul remark about not transacting work via the bedroom. No wonder you lashed out at me!'

'I thought you were going to hit me back!'

'I wasn't in control and knew I had to get out fast,' he confessed. 'But, when I'd no intention of returning to London that night, twenty minutes of pacing my carpet was sufficient to know that next door to you was still too close.'

'You were still upset?' she questioned wonderingly, her trust in him blossoming.

'And how!' he muttered. 'On Monday,' he went on, 'I gave Yolland's application priority attention and, that out of the way, started to get myself sorted out. By Tuesday morning I thought I'd got most of the answers, but, when I'd intended to drive down Tuesday night, I discovered I couldn't wait that long to speak to you— so I rang you at your office that afternoon.'

'You must have thought me dreadful.'

'I think you're fantastic, as it happens, but at that time I came off the phone too steaming angry with you to get my PA to ring Yolland and put him out of his misery. From there I went from furious to sick in my stomach and back to furious again—and determined not to seek you out.'

'I'm sorry,' Pernelle thought she should state. She had been in an emotional uproar herself—it amazed her that Hunter had suffered in the same way.

'By Friday,' Hunter went on, giving her shoulders a squeeze, 'I'd received Yolland's handwritten "thank you", but never suspected, until I drove down that afternoon, that you weren't at work to type it for him.'

'You came down yesterday afternoon?'

'And nearly went into heart failure when I saw that For Sale board in your garden. With the memory of my last phone call to you still haunting me, though, I decided against ringing you at the office to find out what was going on. But when you weren't home by seven I was in such a state of agitation that I found Yolland's home number and rang him.'

'You rang Mike?' she exclaimed.

Hunter nodded. 'And a lot of good it did me. You'd gone to Yeovil,' he said. 'No, he didn't have the address, and no, he didn't know your mother's name now that she'd remarried.'

'Oh, Hunter!' Pernelle gasped, realising that had he had her mother's new name he'd most likely have telephoned her in Yeovil yesterday—or perhaps even come in person.

'Even the estate agent, when I tracked him down, had no idea where you were either,' he shook her by revealing. 'I, sweet love, have been stewing ever since then, waiting, looking and listening for the sound of your car today.'

'Oh!' she sighed, and, while he kept a firm hold of her with one arm round her shoulders, he stretched out a hand and took hold of her hands in her lap.

Then, looking deeply into her melting brown eyes, he asked, 'Have I got it completely wrong? Can it be, my dear, dear Pernelle, that you love me more than "a tiny bit"?' Words were bursting in her to be said, but a stray wisp of shyness held them back, and Hunter pressed on, 'Can it be, as I started to think when I'd got some thinking power back, that you were so emotionally wound up at what was happening between us last Sunday night that you spoke without...'

But at that moment Pernelle grabbed at all her courage. 'I spoke the way I did,' she interrupted softly, 'because I was scared that you'd guessed—er—how it was with me. I thought,' she managed to get some more words out, 'in quite a panic, that I had to hide it. I thought you'd seen that...' She broke off, tripped up by the self-same shyness.

But now she had confessed as much as she had, Hunter wanted more, much more. 'That——?' he prompted urgently—and, in view of all he'd been at pains to tell her in his efforts to gain her trust, Pernelle smiled and, sunbeams bursting inside, could hold back no longer.

'That, with everything that's in me, I love you,' she whispered.

'My love!' Hunter exclaimed hoarsely, and gathered her to him.

With both his arms round her he held her close up against his heart, and to Pernelle it was heaven. She was enchanted by the look of utter joy on his face when, from holding her tightly to him, he pulled back to look into her face as if hardly daring to believe it.

Tenderly then he kissed her, then drew back to look at her again, then to kiss her with light, gentle, adoring kisses. Then he pulled back once more. 'You're sure?' he asked.

'Oh, yes, yes, yes!' she cried, and glimpsed the exultant look that appeared on his face, the moment before he kissed her again. 'But,' she murmured when she had some breath back, 'I thought you'd already worked out—um—how I felt about you.'

'With what logic you'd left me with, I did my best,' he owned, with a smile that was wonderful to see. 'I went over and over again every conversation I'd ever had with you. Conversations where the real you had shone through, the generous-hearted, good-humoured, sweet and lovely you. We'd got on well then, in fact, enjoyed each other's company, or seemed to. So could it be, I asked myself time and time again, that on those other occasions, those occasions when we had hate sessions going full throttle, that you too were trying to hide what was really in your heart?'

'I've thought several times that you were much too clever by half,' Pernelle told him with an enchanted chuckle—and was soundly and thoroughly kissed, for her sauce.

She was feeling a little shaken from the headiness of his kisses, she owned, when at last Hunter pulled back, and he seemed not quite himself too, she saw as he seemed to need to take a steadying breath.

'That—gave me another clue,' he told her, his voice sounding a trifle thick in his throat.

'What?' she questioned, not wondering, since he had just kissed her senseless, that she didn't comprehend what he meant.

'Without question you don't respond freely to the amorous persuasions of the men you date,' he itemised. 'So what was I to think, my love, when, on those rare and wonderful moments I've held you in my arms, your response has been so delightfully uninhibited? Now why, I asked, was that?'

Shyly she laughed. 'Did I give myself totally away?'

'Not entirely totally,' he replied softly, and placed a light and gentle kiss on her mouth. 'But I did have one other clue.'

'Oh, no—what did I do?' she questioned, unable to think where else she had inadvertently fallen down.

Hunter laughed in delight at her expression, then revealed, 'It was last Sunday that, having seen you mowing your lawn from my study, I came down to my sitting-room just as you'd finished de-clogging your mower—then my phone rang.' Oh, no, Pernelle thought, and realised that with everything so absolutely wonderful happening—her trust in Hunter grown so complete—she had, unbelievably, forgotten all about *her*! 'You obviously thought it was your phone. Yet, when I answered my phone, to my tremendous surprise—and against what I was sure was not your normal kind of behaviour—I could swear that you'd deliberately abandoned your mowing to tune in to what I was saying.'

'I——' she began, but had no cover. She couldn't even lie to him, not any more. So she closed her mouth and just looked steadily at him—and still loved him when his face suddenly lit up with amusement.

'Will you forgive me, my darling,' he asked, 'that I was more teasing to my ten-year-old niece than usual?'

'Niece?' she exclaimed, the sun all at once out again. 'I hate you,' she told him lovingly—but had to join in with him when he burst out laughing.

Then, 'Don't hate me, sweet love. It was your reaction to that phone call that later gave me hope that you might, since you'd taken to eavesdropping, be interested in me.'

'I was greener than green about Lily,' she admitted.

'I rather wish now that I'd given in to the feeling of wanting to take you with me to the family celebration last Sunday,' he confessed.

'You had a family celebration last Sunday?' Pernelle asked, the whole of her being feeling warmed that he'd felt like taking her with him.

'It was my parents' fortieth wedding anniversary,' he revealed. 'I hadn't forgotten about the ruby wedding party, but Lily, precocious baggage, wanted to ring to remind me. Anyhow, my darling, I didn't take you with me last Sunday because I didn't want my folks making more of it than there was, but——' he paused, and looked steadily into her eyes as he added '—we'll go and see my parents tomorrow—if that's all right with you?'

Suddenly her heart, which had been beating in a most excited fashion since she'd heard his voice behind her on the drive, began to race furiously. Somehow it seemed to her that Hunter was asking something more than that! 'Er—that's fine,' she answered, 'but...'

'I'm being selfish wanting to show you off to my family,' he cut in quickly and immediately offered, 'We'll go and see your folks first.'

'My folks?' she questioned, and realised that she must have looked confused, but Hunter lightly touched his lips to hers.

Then, his eyes fixed steadily on hers, 'My darling,' he said quietly, 'you've already stated that this place isn't big enough for the two of us. But it could be if we knocked the dividing wall out—and turned the two cottages into one. We've plenty of land we can extend on to, if need be.'

'What . . .' She paused to take a shaky breath. 'What are you saying?'

'My love, I know I'm probably doing this badly—but heaven help me, it's so outside my experience. But I know now that what is lacking in my life is you—the woman I love. So, having found you, I'm not letting you go. I want to live with you, to have you move in with me, to move in with you. I want to come home at night to where you'll be, to love you, to be with you, my darling. I want to marry you.'

'Oh, Hunter!' Pernelle cried. 'That sounds— beautiful!'

'You'll marry me, then?' he questioned—just as though he would not believe it until she gave him a straightforward yes.

'Yes—I will,' she murmured softly.

Hunter let go a pent-up breath. 'Thank God!' he breathed, and seemed about to haul her up close when he questioned, 'And you'll cancel your theatre date tonight?'

'Theatre date?'

'With your friend Julian!'

'Oh,' she said, and realising that Hunter sounded jealous, 'Um—actually, I lied a little. Well, a lot, actually,' she confessed, and then owned, 'I don't—um—have a date with Julian tonight.'

Hunter looked adoringly at her. 'Wretched woman,' he berated her. 'Come here and be kissed!'

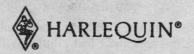

THE TAGGARTS OF TEXAS!

Harlequin's Ruth Jean Dale brings you
THE TAGGARTS OF TEXAS!

Those Taggart men—strong, sexy and hard to resist...

You've met Jesse James Taggart in FIREWORKS!
Harlequin Romance #3205 (July 1992)

Now meet Trey Smith—he's THE RED-BLOODED YANKEE!
Harlequin Temptation #413 (October 1992)

Then there's Daniel Boone Taggart in SHOWDOWN!
Harlequin Romance #3242 (January 1993)

And finally the Taggarts who started it all—in LEGEND!
Harlequin Historical #168 (April 1993)

Read all the Taggart romances!
Meet all the Taggart men!

Available wherever Harlequin books are sold.

• HARLEQUIN •
HISTORICAL •

CHRISTMAS

• STORIES • 1992 •

Capture the magic and romance of Christmas in the 1800s
with HARLEQUIN HISTORICAL CHRISTMAS STORIES
1992—a collection of three stories by celebrated
historical authors. The perfect Christmas gift!

Don't miss these heartwarming stories, available in
November wherever Harlequin books are sold:

**MISS MONTRACHET REQUESTS by Maura Seger
CHRISTMAS BOUNTY by Erin Yorke
A PROMISE KEPT by Bronwyn Williams**

Plus, this Christmas you can also receive a FREE
keepsake Christmas ornament. Watch for details in all
November and December Harlequin books.

**DISCOVER THE ROMANCE AND MAGIC OF THE
HOLIDAY SEASON WITH HARLEQUIN HISTORICAL
CHRISTMAS STORIES!**

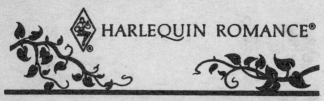

HARLEQUIN ROMANCE®

Valerie Bloomfield comes home to Orchard Valley, Oregon, for the saddest of reasons. Her father has suffered a serious heart attack, and now his three daughters are gathering at his side, praying he'll survive.

Orchard Valley

This visit home will change Valerie's life—especially when she meets Colby Winston, her father's handsome and strong-willed doctor!

"The Orchard Valley trilogy features three delightful, spirited sisters and a trio of equally fascinating men. The stories are rich with the romance, warmth of heart and humor readers expect, and invariably receive, from Debbie Macomber."

—Linda Lael Miller

Don't miss the Orchard Valley trilogy by Debbie Macomber:

VALERIE   Harlequin Romance #3232 (November 1992)
STEPHANIE   Harlequin Romance #3239 (December 1992)
NORAH   Harlequin Romance #3244 (January 1993)

Look for the special cover flash on each book!

Available wherever Harlequin books are sold   ORC-G